THE EDGE

THE EDGE

by Ben Bo

LERNER SPORTS

A DIVISION OF LERNER PUBLISHING GROUP

This book is available in two editions:
Library binding by Lerner Publications Company,
a division of Lerner Publishing Group
Soft cover by First Avenue Editions,
an imprint of Lerner Publishing Group
241 First Avenue North
Minneapolis, MN 55401 U.S.A.

Website address: www.lernerbooks.com

First published in Great Britain in 1998
Bloomsbury Publishing Plc, 38 Soho Square, London W1V 5DF

Copyright © Text Ben Bo 1998

Cover design by Zachary Marell

Library of Congress Cataloging-in-Publication Data
Bo, Ben.
  The edge / by Ben Bo.
    p.   cm.
  Summary: A teenaged gang member accused of various crimes finds redemption working and snowboarding at a ski lodge in the mountains surrounding Canada's Glacier National Park.
  ISBN 0-8225-3307-3 (lib. bdg. : alk. paper)
  ISBN 0-8225-0967-9 (pbk. : alk. paper)
  [1. Self-esteem—Fiction. 2. Snowboarding Fiction. 3. Mountain life — Canada Fiction. 4. Canada Fiction.] I. Title.
PZ7.B7294Ed 1999
[Fic]—dc20   99-20027

Manufactured in the United States of America
2 3 4 5 6 7 – SB – 07 06 05 04 03 02

For John and K

Declan cut his snowboard into the fresh powder, digging in on the edge where the wind had sculpted faces in the ice. The pale, twisted faces of his friends. Jaz, Jamal, Tony and B. J. Hanging far out beyond the supporting rock, screaming silently into the abyss.

"You knew I would come back *here*, didn't you?" he said, calm now. "Suppose you always did."

Silence. Only the wind. Their lifeless eyes staring. Watching. Waiting to see what he would do.

A few yards from the curling nose of his board the slope ended abruptly, dropping away to the snow-covered rocks below. This was it. The Howling Wolf. The ultimate run.

Twenty yards of air down to fresh snow lying at an angle too radical to be called a slope. A sick 90-degree turn into the beast's mouth. Sliding between the razor-edged rocks, a double row of jagged teeth drooling diamond ice, then on down a gully-gullet so narrow and sheer there could be no mistake. No error. It was fly or die when you were swallowed by the Wolf.

And suddenly he knew his whole life had been about this moment. Everything he had ever done had just taken him one step closer to the edge. As if somehow—even before he was born—he had been marked down for the test. Tagged. Just as surely as if his name had been burned into the brick wall of life by some Graffiti-Or-Die artist.

"OK, you win," he said. "So let's do it!"

"Do it! Do it! Do it!" the dead seemed to call.

But it was only his own voice echoing back to him. Over and over. Until it was easy to believe that he was one of the pale, twisted creatures that his friends had become, and had been ever since that terrible night down on the tracks.

He shivered, touched by invisible fingers.

High up on the slope behind, he could see sliders cutting down from the ridge they called the Razor Back. Slashing deep lines in the snow. Zigzagging as they worked down the sheer white face. It was Big Foot and the others. Coming for him.

Too late.

He turned away, but as he did, he caught a glimpse of the mountains as he had once seen them. Shimmering in the sunlight. Piled up like awesome waves with foaming white crests splashing glacial drops at the sky. Rolling endlessly toward some half-imagined shore. A bright clean place he longed to find. A place where no one had ever heard his name and he could be free. Happy again.

It had only been a dream.

"Life sucks," he said. Then louder, "You taught

me that, Jaz." He paused. Took a deep breath and was ready. "So I guess I'll see you guys later!"

"Later! Later! Later!" they shrieked.

He shifted his weight, pulling the nose of his board around. He felt it come alive again beneath his feet. Suddenly electric. Crackling on the ice as he slid down the slope toward the edge.

1

Declan was at the wall again. Down by the tracks. Working on the crumbling bricks in front of him, a spray can in each hand. Lost. Drifting in a different dimension inside his head. Slashing through the grime with razor cuts of pure color.

He worked quickly. Each color as bright and vibrant as the one before. Silver, blue, and black slashed with crimson red. His fingers shooting vapor jet trails that formed into shapes on the crumbling canvas before his eyes.

"You're burning my bricks, man," a voice said suddenly.

Startled, Declan instinctively dropped the bomb of spray paint and kicked it away from him into the grass. He turned slowly.

The kid was bigger, broader, and taller. He wore his checked woolen cap turned back to front and his baggy trousers were torn at the knees. He looked as if he had slept in his leather jacket.

Declan looked around for a way out, but could see he was trapped. Caught on the wrong side of the tracks. His back up against the grimy wall that ran alongside the Fraser Highway. The kid's restless eyes flicked to the word burned into the wall in big, fat letters: REJECT. Declan moved away, disowning his tag quickly.

The other's eyes narrowed into dangerous slits.

"I know you," he said, "you're that new kid just moved in on Whitebark Avenue."

"I gotta go," Declan said, grabbing his backpack. He slung it over his shoulder and picked up his skateboard from where it lay in the tufts of coarse grass at the side of the track.

"Not so fast!" The kid took a step nearer. His eyes flicked down to the skateboard then back to the word on the wall. "These tracks belong to the UXTs. Everyone knows that."

"I didn't—sorry," Declan lied.

He had seen the tags on the walls. JAZ, JAM THE MAN, TBONE, and BADJ. The names of the URBAN XTREME TEAM cut in the concrete, colored silver, blue, and red and edged in black. Their places marked in the crumbling decay that surrounded them.

That's why Declan had come. Climbing over the broken wall and jumping down into the mist that swirled around the tracks. Down to that cold, forgotten place where the air smelt of burnt newspaper and where dead leaves, as wrinkled as old men's hands, clawed at a sky lost to them forever. That's why he tagged himself REJECT, as if by adding his name to the others on that wall he would become part of something. Part of them.

"The way I see it," the kid said, "that's our wall so you owe us," he searched for a word, then smiled, "*rent.*"

Declan had only been in Vancouver a week but he had already seen and heard enough about the UXTs at school to know he was in a dangerous game. This kid—he thought he was

Jaz—was crazy. "Big trouble." "Bad news." Every-one at Bear Creek High School said so. But there was also something cool about him. Something bold and confident that Declan couldn't help liking.

"I don't have any money," Declan said, truthfully.

He turned out the pockets of his jeans and his padded jacket. Jaz dismissed the few cents De-clan produced and rummaged through Declan's backpack instead, shaking the half-empty cans of spray paint he found. Listening to the ball bear-ings as they click-clacked inside to see if the cans were full. Discarding each in turn, along with any books he accidentally pulled out.

"Books are junk, man!" he said in a voice that sounded tired of saying it.

"Yeah, right!" Declan said, dropping the book he had retrieved from the mess of litter. He wiped his hand on the back of his jeans as if frightened some of the words might have rubbed off, stick-ing to his fingers to give him away.

So the kid, Jaz, took the skateboard instead. Running his fingers along the flat of the board. Spinning the wheels until they fizzed loudly. "Now this is more like it," he said.

"No way!"

"Relax, man," Jaz said, pushing him hard.

Caught by surprise, Declan stumbled, tripped, and fell. He landed in the tufty grass with a thump that made his teeth clack.

Jaz grinned down at him. "Your first lesson—life sucks. Remember that!"

Defeated, Declan could only sit and watch as

Jaz turned and walked away.

Jaz climbed up on to the wall, where he stood for a moment, the board resting easily on one hip, silhouetted against the pale gray of the wintery sky. A statue. Victorious.

Declan heard him laugh.

"Later, man!" Jaz said, and was gone.

"What do you mean you *lost* it?"

"I just did, that's all."

Declan sat at the table in the kitchen and shifted under the weight of his mother's stare. That board had cost a lot and she wasn't happy.

"Did you know they named a movie after the Clouded Yellow?" his dad asked, holding up a large yellow butterfly skewered on the end of a silver pin. "Starred Trevor Howard, I think."

A sharp intake of breath. A pause. Then: "I don't know what I've done to deserve the pair of you!" eventually exploded out of his mother. "I have a husband who's at home all day pinning bugs to a board instead of looking for a job. And a son who lives in a dream world."

Declan knew what was coming next. It was the, "Why can't you be normal like other kids?" lecture.

He sat at the kitchen table and listened without hearing. Letting it all wash over him until he was relieved by the shrill tone of her mobile phone. Business. He marveled at the smooth way her voice changed when she answered that phone. One moment she could be going ballistic, the next, she was calm and in control.

Another rented house, flat boarded, white and neat behind its front lawn. Another city suburb. Another school. Another life. He drifted through the changes his mother's company forced upon them as if it was all happening to someone else. A bad dream he supposed he should be used to by now, but wasn't.

He remembered his first glimpse of Vancouver. It had been from the window of an Air Canada jet, flying in from Toronto. The city was laid out in neat blocks below, spreading up the Fraser River on to the wooded slopes of the mountains that surrounded it. Downtown growing heavy with high rises as they descended. Banking over Vancouver Island with one wing dipped toward the cranes lining the docks.

"Our new home," his mother had said.

Declan sat at the kitchen table and watched his dad pin the Clouded Yellow to a board and begin fitting the frame.

His mother ended the call and picked up where she had left off. "So you had better shape up or you'll be on the scrap heap at forty, just like your father. . . ."

He remembered a time when he had enjoyed helping his father with his hobby of collecting insects. Pinning butterflies and beetles to boards in neat lines according to size. Tagging them with their strange, unfamiliar Latin names, then framing them in glass boxes. His mother accepted the butterflies, but not the scorpions, spiders, or the giant stag beetles. These were always kept hidden away in a drawer.

"You know what your mother thinks about arachnids, Champ," his father always said.

Which had given Declan the idea of borrowing

that dead tarantula. For a while, he used it to devastating effect. Deliberately leaving it lying around for her to find. Waiting for her screams for help—*his* help—before he came running. He enjoyed nothing better than being able to rescue her. Until the day she caught on to what he was doing. That wiped the smile off his face.

"I've got schoolwork to do," he said, scraping back his chair.

For reasons he couldn't explain, he found he could no longer bear to watch those butterflies being pinned to a board. So he made his way upstairs and kicked his bedroom door shut behind him. Ignoring the books on his desk, he pulled out the ragged pad of paper he kept hidden under his bed.

He leafed through the drawings inside until he reached one he hadn't finished. It was of a crowd jostling in a room. Drawn faces, strained and staring. Some standing. Some sitting. All with mobile phones ringing in their ears.

He picked up a stub of pencil and smoothed the paper flat before starting to draw. With quick, strong strokes, he began to sketch, blocking in the form with shades of black and gray.

And slowly another figure appeared on the page. A boy with butterfly wings. Nailed to the wall. Tagged. Tongue lolling out of his mouth as if the life had been choked out of him just as he had spread his wings to fly.

3

Declan first noticed the Indian totem poles on his way to school.

Three of them, with carved heads and fierce, staring eyes. As tall as trees, they stood around the park gates like three brightly painted giants gathered together in the watery March sunshine.

He knew as soon as he saw them that they were special. They spoke to him without the need for anything as ordinary as words, and he found an age of wisdom in their fiery eyes. He supposed that was why they had been left to guard the park against the approach of the concrete and glass that surrounded it.

So he stopped there every morning on his way to school. Greeting each by the names he had given them: Charlie, Big Bird, and Sad Face. Dwarfed by their great size, yet feeling strangely tall, as if just being with them made him special too. A friend.

And that morning was no different from any other. Until he saw Jaz.

Declan wasn't sure if it was him at first, so he climbed the slope through the trees for a better look. Then he recognized the cap and the skateboard.

Jaz was doing tricks on the skate ramp in the corner of the park. The wheels of the board rumbling on the concrete as he rolled from side to side across the flattened U-shape of the halfpipe. Kicking off the lip. Turning in the air. Swooping down again to land in the trough before shooting up the other side to blast off once more. Swinging like the pendulum of a clock that had long ago become careless of time.

"What do you want?" Jaz said, jumping off the ramp.

"My board back."

Jaz's quick eyes flicked down to the board, then back up to study Declan's face. "Reject!" he said, recognizing him. He grinned slyly. "But how do I know it's yours?"

"You took it, remember!" Declan said. "And anyway that's my name on the bottom—Declan Murray."

Jaz shook his head. "Nope! Still don't believe you," he said. "Guess you'll just have to prove it."

"And how am I going to do that?"

Jaz nodded down the slope at a park bench under an old maple tree, halfway down. "Grind its nose along the back of that seat and maybe I'll believe you."

It was more than just a difficult jump. From where Declan stood, it looked like suicide or, at the very least, a stay in the hospital.

"Of course, once you're on the board you could keep right on going," Jaz said, casually. "If you're too chicken, that is."

The thought had entered Declan's head, too, but he put it out of his mind. "OK," he said, "if that's what it takes."

Jaz slapped him on the back. "Do it, man!"

Declan kicked off, picking up speed as he dropped down the steeply sloping path. Timing his run better than he dared hope, he flicked up the nose of his board and made the jump onto the back of the bench. He connected briefly— more by luck than skill—shifted his weight onto his front foot and pressed the underside of his board into the wood of the bench. Then suddenly he was bouncing off the end in a shower of flaking green paint.

"Too easy, man," Jaz called down to him.

"Like to see you do better," Declan said as he climbed back up the slope.

"OK," was all Jaz said but there was a strange look in his eyes.

Declan followed his gaze, past Charlie, Big Bird, and Sad Face, through the gate, across the road to the steps that fanned out on the other side. There were twenty of them at least, dropping down between the buildings to a small fountain in a square surrounded by shops below.

"You're crazy!" he whispered.

Jaz just laughed. "Who needs a life anyway?"

Declan could only stand and watch as Jaz set off down the slope. He hit the street fast. Too fast. Scattering the people on their way to work. Brakes squealed. A car swerved but he seemed oblivious of the chaos he caused. Immune to the danger. Indestructible.

Jaz blasted off the top step. One hand thrown up like a rodeo star. The other gripping the edge of the board. And for one stretched moment he seemed able to rise above the buildings that crowded in all around. Flying high, free, until the city reached up and dragged him down once more.

Jaz hit the ground hard, smacking into the concrete. The impact tearing the wheels off the back of the board. The tail dropped, sending him spinning away as the board disintegrated, just another piece of city litter caught by the wind.

Declan was running long before he saw Jaz hit the low wall of the fountain. He crossed the road and took the steps four at a time. A small crowd had already gathered at the bottom. A semicircle of people stared down at Jaz, lying among the shattered remains of the skateboard. His eyes were closed. A thin trail of blood trickled from a cut on his forehead.

"Jeez, Jaz—are you OK?" Declan said, dropping to his knees.

Jaz opened one eye. "You can have your board back now," he said, a big grin splitting his face.

"Should have seen your face, man!"

"I was worried about my board," Declan hissed. "Look at it! It's totaled."

"Piece of crap anyway," Jaz said, kicking the pieces so they went spinning away. "Come on. Let's split."

Declan glanced over his shoulder. The little crowd had begun to drift way, disappointed. No blood. No guts. Just a couple of kids messing around. Nothing.

"What about school?" he asked.

"School's for droids, man!" Jaz said. "We've got more important stuff to do, right?"

Declan thought for a moment, hovering on the edge of a decision not to go, then made up his mind. "Right."

Jaz spotted the others hanging around the corner near the closed-down bakery. Jamal, Tony, and B. J. sitting on a wall that sprouted graffiti like a big, matted creeper.

"Who's he?" asked Jamal, flicking the smoldering butt of his cigarette into the litter and leaves the wind was chasing around the gutter.

"This is Declan," Jaz said, "otherwise known as *Reject*."

The name caused quite a stir. Jamal's eyes flashed in his dark brown face as he stood up. Tony and B. J. moved around to stand on either side. For one horrible moment, Declan wondered whether he had walked into a trap.

"Leave it! He's cool," Jaz said.

"But he's been burning our bricks," Jamal said. "You going to let him get away with that?"

"It would be OK if he was a UXT, right?" Jaz waited for them all to nod. "Good, because Declan has just joined up."

Jamal frowned. "Who says?"

"I do. You got a problem with that, man?" Jaz's voice was quiet. His words were edged in steel.

They squared up to one another, each searching for a sign of weakness in the other's eyes.

They were both big, about the same height and weight, and seemed equally matched. Even so, Jamal looked away first.

He glared at Declan. "The UXTs don't carry no passengers—you got that, new boy?"

Declan nodded.

It wasn't long before they put him to the test.

They hit Fat Arnold's Hardware Store just before midday.

The sliding glass doors shuddered open before them as they walked up, allowing a faint odor of stale tobacco and sweat to escape.

Beneath the starburst shapes of faded, cardboard signs, a dozen aisles stretched away in front of them. The metal shelves were piled high with boxes of nails and nuts and bolts, pots of paint, plastic pipes, and rolls of electrical wire in every size. And at the far end, stacked up neatly, a whole rainbow in spray cans.

"Every color you've ever wanted and then some," Jaz whispered. "All you gotta do is help yourself."

He made it sound easy. Jaz was good at that.

"What about her?" Declan asked, pointing to the gray-haired woman watching them suspiciously from behind the counter.

"You leave her to me," Jaz said. "Just do what the others do. Grab as many paint bombs as you can, then get out fast. Don't stop for no one." He waited for Declan to nod. "And relax, man. We meet at eight down at the tracks."

"Shouldn't you boys be in school?" the woman asked, peering at Jaz over the thick frames of her halfmoon spectacles.

"It's Career Development Day," Jaz lied easily.

She laughed but her eyes didn't. "Well, you're wasting your time in this neighborhood," she said. "You won't find any careers developing around here—unless you count sitting around reading the newspaper. Ain't that right, Arnold?" She said the last part over her shoulder in a loud voice.

A grunt from the little office at the back. A wooden chair leg scraped on the floor. The sound of a newspaper being hidden in a place too small for it. Then silence.

It was too easy. She couldn't watch them all at the same time. Jaz kept her busy with a steady flow of questions about what it was like to have a job, while Jamal, Tony, and B. J. just helped themselves. With quick, practiced fingers, they snatched up the cans, stripping the shelves bare, stuffing them away until their pockets were bulging.

"Do it!" a breathless voice whispered. "Do it!"

Declan heard it clearly. But it wasn't Jaz's, Jamal's, Tony's, nor B. J.'s. It sounded like his own voice, echoing out of some dark place within him. As if somewhere, deep inside, there lurked another Declan longing to break free.

He saw his hand begin to move. He watched it as if it belonged to someone else. Reaching out.

Stretching until he felt the touch of cool metal on his fingertips. And all the while the voice was whispering in his head. Telling him what to do.

Until suddenly it changed and became someone else's: "You thieving little punk!" it snarled, as Fat Arnold's big, sweaty face crowded into his.

Declan gasped as stale breath washed over him. A giant hand twisted into his collar and shook him until he thought his brain would fall out.

"I got one, Martha!" Fat Arnold bellowed. "Call the police!"

The hardware store dissolved into a blur before Declan's eyes.

Everything seemed to be happening at once. He flapped about helplessly, hooked on his collar, catching glimpses of the others as they dodged this way and that. He could hear shouts and someone gabbling words into a telephone. Harsh words clashed like cymbals in his ears.

Vaguely, he wondered who the dirty, little thief was, the one they had caught stealing, the animal who should be locked up for good. Then slowly the truth began to dawn on him. It shredded the mist that fogged his brain and he began to feel sick. Dizzy. His head spinning as if he had stumbled to the very edge of some bottomless hole and was about to fall shrieking to his doom.

"No! Please!" he begged. "I didn't mean to. You've got to let me go!"

But Fat Arnold just laughed until his chins wobbled. "Tell it to the judge, sonny!"

Declan panicked and kicked out. He heard a grunt as his foot found the kettledrum that was Fat Arnold's bulging stomach. The grip on his collar slackened. He dropped down low. Twisted sharply. And suddenly he was free. Running down the aisles between the metal shelves, with rolls of electrical wire in every size going the other way.

Just the thought of what he had done made Declan feel cold and hollow inside.

He relived it over and over. That terrible moment in Fat Arnold's store. The moment when he had been caught stealing. The moment he had let the others down.

All he had to do was take a few cans of paint. How difficult could that be? It wasn't as if he had been asked to eat a whole raw cow backward. But he had just stood there, frozen to the spot like he had been iced.

What a loser! he thought miserably.

He poked at the vegetables on his plate. His mother had telephoned at the last minute to say she was held up at the office, so the supper his dad had cooked was burnt around the edges.

"I hate rabbit food," he said.

"Vegetables are good for you, Champ. They'll help you grow up big and strong."

"How big? As big as a totem pole? As big as a building? As big as the world?"

"No, of course not."

"Then it's stupid! So stop talking to me like I'm a kid!"

A pause.

"Is there something wrong, Champ?"

"And stop calling me that stupid name!"

Declan snapped, slamming his fork into the pile of carrots. He almost knocked over his chair in his hurry to get out of the kitchen and up to the solitude of his room.

He sat at his desk, drawing tortured faces then scrubbing them out again, wishing he could think of a way to show the others he was sorry for what he had done. He was just wondering how other people proved their friendship for one another when he had an idea.

His heart began to beat faster as he ran his finger along the row of books on the shelf in front of him. He stopped at the one about famous painters—the one he had bought at a second-hand shop for only two dollars—and pulled it out. Flicking through the pages he quickly found what he was looking for: a picture of Vincent Van Gogh with a bandage wrapped around his head; a hollow-cheeked man with haunting, green eyes that had always reminded him of his own.

He did *that* for a friend, he thought.

Declan noticed the scissors in the jar on his desk and picked them up. They were for cutting paper, blunt-nosed and not very sharp, but he was sure they would do. He snapped them open and closed several times to make sure they worked properly, then stood up and looked at himself in the mirror.

The metal felt cold against his skin as he traced the blades down the pink curves and whorls of his ear. He stopped when he reached the soft fleshiness of his earlobe. The blades caught the light as they came apart. He watched, fascinated, as the little flap of skin slipped helplessly into the jaws. Sliding along the sharpened edges until it jammed at the point where the blades met.

He tried to swallow, but his tongue seemed super-glued to the roof of his mouth. His heart was thumping as he closed his eyes and squeezed.

"You OK, Cham . . . Declan?" his dad asked, knocking at the door.

Startled, Declan opened his eyes, realized what he was about to do, and dropped the scissors quickly. He backed away from his own reflection, staring at his uncut earlobe in horror.

The knock came at the door again and sent him diving onto his bed, burrowing under the covers to lie still just as the door opened. He held his breath and pretended to be asleep. Moments later he heard the door close again quietly.

7:45 p.m.

Declan opened his bedroom window and slipped out into the darkness. He swung out onto the gutter, feet kicking at the air, caught hold of the drainpipe, and slid down to land with a soft thud in the flowerbed below. He pulled up the padded collar of his jacket and set off down the road, his breath frosting on the chill night air.

He reached the wall by the Fraser Highway at exactly 8 o'clock, climbed up, and jumped down to the railway line on the other side.

"You there, Jaz?" he called softly.

No reply.

Nearby an engine was moving freight, the couplings clanking as the boxcars passed in and out of the bright cones of light dropped by the lopsided spotlights in the railyard. Somewhere in the distant streets a dog was barking. A police siren wailed, rising and falling, fading into the city night.

He pulled out his torch and sent the ragged shadows scuttling away to hide from its light, the pencil-thin beam picking out his tag on the wall and the glint of the empty spray cans lying in the scrubby grass.

He moved on, the circle of light bobbing about on the ground in front of him as he followed the path, until he reached a footbridge that arched awkwardly over the tracks. Here, he paused to listen, alert to the scuffling sounds of the night.

He spotted something moving on the other side of the bridge and crept closer. An old coat was hanging, torn and tattered, on the razor wire that curled along the top of a padlocked gate barring his way. One sleeve flapping in the freshening breeze, beckoning to him like Ahab's arm.

Beyond the gate he could just make out a jumble of shadows. Factories and warehouses whose roofs cut a jagged line against the sky. Pitch black against the sky that was poisoned orange by the glow of a million city street lamps.

Suddenly a shadow came up over the handrail of the bridge and snatched his torch from his hand. He almost took off with fright as the beam blinked off abruptly.

"Quick!" It was Jaz's voice. "Down here—before Pluto nails you!"

Jaz's shadow dropped back out of sight, melting into the others below the bridge just as the powerful beam of another torch cut the night. Someone was coming around the corner of one of the buildings on the other side of the gate.

Declan slipped over the handrail and stood peering down into the black hole. It was too dark to see the ground below. He hesitated until he felt the cold metal of the bridge seeping through his jeans into the backs of his legs, then he took a deep breath and plunged into the unknown.

Declan landed in the deep shadows by the side of the track and crouched in the scrubby grass. He listened, wondering what to do next.

"Stay down!" Jaz warned.

The bloated moon came out from behind a cloud, its cold, clear light turning the tracks to liquid silver before it disappeared again, allowing the shadows to creep back even darker than before.

A chain rattled and the hinges of the gate groaned with rust. Declan held his breath as a finger of light pointed down from the bridge above, poking into the shadows around them. It jabbed this way and that, then jumped back onto the bridge and pointed the way across to the other side.

"Pluto?" Declan asked in a whisper when the light had gone.

Jaz nodded. "Old man Roper—the security guard. But we call him Pluto because he's king of this underworld."

"How do you mean?"

"Read this dumb book once," Jaz explained. "It was all about these gods the Romans had. One for just about everything. Even one who ruled a place where all these crazy ghosts hung out. They called it the Underworld." Jaz looked about.

"Figure it must've been just like this."

"You mean there are ghosts down here!"

"Only us," Jaz said, but he did not laugh. "Anyway, old man Roper's got this killer dog just like the god-dude in the book. That's why we started calling him Pluto—the name just stuck."

Declan peered nervously into the shadows around him. "What does it look like, the dog I mean?"

"You'll know when you see it," Jaz said. "It'll be the one with its teeth in your throat."

They moved on quickly after that. Following the tracks. Picking their way between the criss-crossed rails, keeping to the concrete sleepers wherever possible so their feet did not crunch on the deep, stony ballast in between. Avoiding the high voltage cables that hummed softly in the darkness.

Soon, however, the tracks began to untangle themselves into straight lines, passing under a series of concrete bridges to disappear into the inky blackness of a tunnel. There solid walls leapt out of the ground on either side. Sloping at steep angles. Trapping the moon in a strip of starless sky above.

Jaz risked a light.

"So you made it then," Jamal said, as he stepped out from behind a bridge support.

He seemed disappointed and deliberately dropped the backpack he was carrying at Declan's feet. The cans of spray paint rattled inside.

"Told you he would," Jaz said, sounding like someone who had won a bet.

Declan could feel the resentment burning out of Jamal like heat and knew that his real test was still to come.

Tony and B. J. appeared out of the darkness, arguing.

"I swear Pluto's dog has got three heads. I reckon it could take out Arnold Schwarzenegger, Jean-Claude Van Damme *and* Segal all at the same time," Tony was saying.

"No way, man," B. J. shook his head. "Not Van Damme—he'd have a rocket launcher..."

The rest was lost in the noise of the freight train that came thundering out of the tunnel. Its lights dazzlingly bright. Its diesel engine screaming as it towed a string of metal ore carriers destined for the waiting ships down at the docks. It shook the ground beneath their feet and sent them staggering back against the wall, the noise sucking the breath right out of their lungs as it passed.

"Come on, we've wasted enough time," Jaz said, shining his torch around at the unmarked walls. "I'm in the mood to burn these clean skins, real bad."

He knelt to unbuckle the backpack and started dealing out the cans inside. The ball-bearings click-clacking as he sent the cans spinning end over end into their eager hands. Black, silver, red, blue, and yellow. All new.

"Don't see why he should get any," Jamal said, pointing at Declan. "We did all the work back there in Fat Arnold's. He just stood there and got himself nailed."

Jaz looked up. "What are you saying, man?"

"I'm saying, I figure this new boy's *chicken*," Jamal said, spitting out the word. He turned to the others. "I'm saying if he wants to join the UXTs he's got to prove he can really cut it—up there on the *face*."

He took the torch and shone it up the sloping wall to a point almost halfway up where it became sheer. A line of weeds marked the joint, clinging to the crack in the concrete, waving gently in the breeze.

Jaz shook his head. "Too risky without a rope, man," he said. "There's no way he could hold on if a big freight like the last one comes bulleting out of that tunnel. He'd slide right down that slope and under the wheels."

"And what do you say, new boy?" Jamal asked.

All eyes were on Declan.

He studied the wall. It was risky all right. But the voice in his head was whispering again.

"I'll do it," he said, quietly. "I'll do it now."

Jaz helped him up the slope as far as he could, then shone the torch for him as he continued to climb. Declan searched out the cracks in the concrete with his fingers. His shoes finding grip on the rough surface. Pulling himself up, hand over hand, as the others commented on his progress from below.

"Space. The final frontier," Tony said. "The UXTs go where no tag man has gone before."

"Well, he better be a good Klingon if a train comes," B. J. said, "otherwise it's going to be, 'Beam me up in a bag, Scotty.' "

Declan tried to ignore them after that. He continued to work his way up, tugging at the weeds until he found ones deeply rooted enough to hold his weight before moving on. He was close to the face now. Very close. It seemed to rise up in front of him for ever. Sheer. Empty.

When he could go no farther, he settled as comfortably as he could and pulled a can of silver spray paint from his pocket. His hand shook as he cleared the nozzle with a quick squirt. He tried to focus on the piece of wall trapped in the circle of light in front of him.

Then a jet of pure silver blasted from the tip of his forefinger onto the crumbling, blank canvas in front of him. Followed by another and another, and slowly he began to relax. His hand moving automatically. All awkwardness forgotten as the colors filled his head. Sweeping in silver arcs. Slashing back at angles in black and red. Tagging that sheer face for the UXTs.

"Listen!" Jaz hissed.

Declan paused. He felt a tremor run through the wall. A trembling. Faint, at first, but growing steadily stronger. Until it became a rumble like that of distant thunder and the wall began to shake.

"Get out of there, man!" he heard Jaz shout.

Too late.

The train came slithering out of the tunnel at terrific speed. Uncoiling itself from that dark hole. Pulling its long, distended body behind it like a monstrous, silver worm that had lived too long in the dark.

Declan felt his feet slipping as the wall bucked under him. He scrabbled for a hold, but the weeds tore out of the face in clumps like coarse, dead hair. He slipped farther, held on for a moment longer, then fell with a terrifying rush.

He hit the ground. Staggered. One step forward took him into the path of the train. The lights were blindingly bright. He tried to shield his eyes, thoughts of escape driven from his head.

The blow, when it came, knocked all the air out of him and sent him spinning back against the wall. The world dissolved into a terrifying rush of wind as the train hurtled past, the boxcars clattering on the track for what seemed like an eternity before everything went black.

When Declan opened his eyes, he found himself lying in the dark by the side of the track. "What happened?" he groaned.

"You almost got yourself sliced and diced, that's what happened," Jaz said.

Declan sat up stiffly and stared at the track only inches from his feet. He moved his legs and was relieved to see his feet were still attached. Both arms too. No blood.

He looked around. "How? I mean, the last thing I remember . . ."

"Jamal pushed you out of the way of the train," Tony explained.

"Jamal?"

"It was no big deal," Jamal said.

"But . . ."

"Forget it!" Jamal insisted. "Like I said, it was no big deal. And anyway, the UXTs always stick together."

They were only words, but somehow they made Declan feel taller. Stronger.

Later, as they made their way back, Declan smiled to himself. He didn't care if it was wrong to be down on those tracks. It didn't even worry him that he had almost been cut to pieces by a train. He was a member of the UXTs and that made everything seem right. And for the first time in his whole life, he felt as if he belonged.

They reached the metal footbridge and waited in the shadows as Jaz climbed up to take a look. Pluto would be nearby and that made them tense. They watched Jaz's silhouette anxiously, hoping for the all-clear.

It came as a soft, breathy whistle—like the call of a night bird—and the tension blew out of them in a rush. They grinned in the half-darkness, racing each other to the top. Swinging through the branching arms of the bridge. Hardly noticing the icy cold of the metal as they slipped over the handrail to stand by the gate. Only then did Declan notice the chain was missing from the gate. It was a trap.

"Freeze!"

"Pluto!"

"Stay where you are, street rats!" the big security guard said, shining his powerful torch into their faces. "Move and I'll set Cerber on you!"

The big Doberman was by his side, straining at the leash, snarling and snapping at the air, ready to go for anyone stupid enough to run.

Pluto spoke into the radio attached to the lapel of his jacket. "Roper. Sector two. Near the old warehouses. Bringing in five." Then he rounded them up and herded them through the gate. He took no chances and locked it securely after them before forcing them on toward the jumble of shadowy buildings nearby.

"I say we take our chances in the warehouses," Jaz whispered out of the corner of his mouth, as he fell in step at Declan's side.

Declan looked at the dog. "Aren't you forgetting something?"

"I'll take care of the hound from hell," Jaz said, slipping the backpack down off his shoulder. "Just be ready to go on the count of three. And remember . . ."

". . . don't stop for no one," Declan finished for him.

Jaz grinned. "Now you're starting to get it, Reject!" he said, beginning the count at, *"Three!"*

They all went together.

Declan ran. He ran faster than he had ever run in his whole life. Feet thumping. Heart pumping. Driven by sheer terror. The beast's breath hot on the back of his neck. But just when he was sure it had him, he saw Jaz stuff the backpack into its jaws and the furious snarl began to fade as they ran on. Free.

"In here!" Jaz said, panting.

He kicked out the rotten planks that had been nailed over a door at the back of one of the buildings and they scrambled inside. He made them slide an old wooden crate across to block the hole and pile junk on top to be sure the dog could not follow.

"Do you think," Declan asked, his breath coming in ragged gasps, "we've shaken them off?"

"Too easy," Jaz decided.

Declan looked around. The smeary windows let in just enough moonlight to see the building was being used as a warehouse to store second-hand furniture. Tables, armchairs, old beds were all piled up together. Some wrapped in plastic sheeting. Most too old and broken to bother. It formed a giant maze easily big enough in which to lose themselves.

"We can hole up in here for a while," Jaz said.

They agreed and moved on. Turning left, then right, then right again. Following the twisting passages between the piles of furniture as they worked their way into the very heart of the building. They reached some rickety, wooden stairs and paused.

"Maybe they lead up onto the roof," Tony said, peering into the gloom above.

"And maybe they don't," Jamal said, digging a pack of cigarettes from his pocket. He put one to his lips and suddenly a match was flaring brightly in the darkness.

"Are you crazy! Put it out!" Jaz said, knocking the match away from the cigarette. It spluttered and died, but the cigarette was already lit.

"I ain't hurting no one," Jamal snarled.

"Don't be a dink," Jaz said. "Pluto won't need a dog to find us if he smells smoke!"

Jamal rolled his eyes. He took a long, defiant drag on the cigarette, then flicked it away still smoldering into the darkness.

It took a moment for them to realize what he had done, then they were all scrambling in the litter on the floor, looking for it.

"You better hope it went out, man," Jaz said, glaring at Jamal when they stood up empty-handed.

But their luck had just run out.

By the time they had made up their minds to try the roof, the cigarette had already smoked itself into a flame in the litter. Suddenly free, the little flame crackled happily, catching on an old rag before jumping up into the stuffing of an arm chair. From that seat, the fire spread with surprising speed.

As Jaz led them up the stairs, they could not see the sparks dancing like fireflies behind them, alighting here and there on the old furniture to explode into fiery yellow blooms.

As they kicked open the door, they did not feel the building shudder as the flames ate into its dusty heart. And as they stepped out onto the flat roof in the moonlight, they did not smell the thick, acrid smoke as it came creeping up the stairs after them, as silent as death.

They knew nothing of the danger below, so they wasted the precious time left to them, hiding among the twisting pipes and big metal chimney vents that crowned the roof of the old building. Until the first thin wisps of smoke started seeping out through the cracks in the broken door.

"Fire!" Declan did not know who said it first, but the word sent a shiver through them all.

The cool night air fanned the flames as Jaz pulled open the door. The heat forced them back as the fire flared up the stairs, yellow tongues licking around the door jamb.

"It wasn't my fault!" Jamal began squealing.

Jaz kicked the door closed and told him to shut up. "Start looking for another way down," he said. "That door won't hold for long now."

So they searched the roof, which stretched wide and flat around them in the moonlight. Milling around the pipes and chimney vents, a flock of wingless birds, lost. But they found no other way down.

A wail of despair welled out of them as they were forced back the way they had come. Running now. Gasping for breath, they tried to dodge the flames that suddenly seemed to be everywhere. Like the fiery fingers of some hideous half-seen beast, the flames snatched at their ankles, reaching higher each time they passed.

Trapped. Stumbling. The smoke filled their eyes with scalding tears, blinding them with panic that took them dangerously close to the edge, then sent them stampeding back, careless of who went down in the rush.

Declan caught his foot on a metal pipe and fell heavily. "Hey, wait for me!" he begged, but they could not hear him above their own shouts.

He scrambled back from the dark void that yawned in front of him until he bumped up against a chimney. There he lay for what seemed like a lifetime before he noticed the flashing lights. He rubbed at the tears that burned his eyes and blinked back at them. Then slowly, he crawled to the edge and looked down.

Far below, the fire engines were already pulling up in front of the warehouses. He counted three of them and more in the distance. Huge red-and-white trucks with silver ladder spines. The doors burst open and men in yellow helmets spilled out.

"Up here!" he croaked, the smoke in his voice. Then louder, "Up h-eee-eee-eeere!"

He waved his arms over his head and saw a fireman stop and point. Others looked. Moments later the message had been passed along the line and the hydraulic ladder on the back of one of the fire engines began to swing in an arc toward him.

"They're coming," he sobbed, looking around for the others. He caught a glimpse of them on the far side of the roof. Jaz, Jamal, Tony, and B. J. Together. Eyes wide and staring. Pale beneath the streaks of soot that caked their cheeks, setting their faces in grimacing death masks. He called out to them, laughing as the tears ran down his cheeks. "It's going to be OK!"

Then the roof collapsed.

It just seemed to open up between them like a big orange mouth breathing flames high into the night sky. Free at last, the fire beast roared, spitting sparks at the moon and cracking its jaws with every exploding timber. Declan felt its burning breath on his face and screamed.

"Jaaaaaaaaaaaaaaaaaaaaaaaaaaaaaaaaaaaaaaaz!"

And all the while, the twisted chimneys stood around like witches in pointed metal hats, casting their spells into the funeral fire.

Declan sat on the bench staring at the door opposite, seeing nothing.

The room was small, beige, with a window that did not open overlooking a yard with a high wall. Two doors: one in, one out. The bench along the wall. And him.

On the other side of that closed door, he could hear the murmur of voices. His mother's mostly. His dad's occasionally. Miss "Call-me-Polly" Everett answering, her tone always understanding and reasonable.

A week had passed since the firefighters had plucked him—and only him—from the burning roof. In the hospital, the nights had been a slow motion of terrible dreams. The days were filled with faces passing in a constant procession. Some serious, some angry, some sad, but all with the same accusing look in their eyes.

"You've got to find the others!" he had shouted to the firefighters running between the fire engines. "Jaz and Jamal and Tony and B. J.! They're up there—on the roof!"

Declan's whole body had shaken until his teeth chattered. He remembered a police officer throwing a blanket around his shoulders like a cape; the feel of the coarse wool prickling on the back of his neck as he was led toward the waiting ambulance. But above all, he remembered the way the firefighters had turned to look as he had passed, their eyes glittering in their soot-blackened faces.

"Dumb kid—should have fried too," one had said, spitting at the fire.

He felt only the numbness after that.

The door opened. Miss Everett, neat in blue and wearing big, round glasses, smiled at him. A practiced smile. He decided she had smiled a million times before.

"Come in Declan," she said. "And remember, I want you to call me Polly."

"Yes, Miss Everett," he said as he stood up.

He stepped into the office and closed the door. He could feel his mother's eyes boring into him from where she stood in the corner, but he did not look at her.

Miss Everett asked him to sit by his father and he obeyed, automatically. Watching her across the desk as she tapped typed sheets marked, "Declan Alastair Murray" into neat piles. Pausing every now and then to make a note in the margin with a red pen.

"The hospital report says you were lucky," she said, looking up at last. "Smoke inhalation. Minor burns. No lasting damage."

Lucky. They had all used that word. The doctors, the nurses, the police. Even that reporter, the one who had called him an animal. Now her.

What did she know? What did any of them know? How could he be lucky when he had lost the only friends he had ever had.

"I'll give him lasting damage," his mother said. She stepped forward and slapped a copy of the *Vancouver Herald* onto the desk in front of him. "Just look at that! It's all over the front page."

Bored stupid. Why our youth is running wild, the headline shouted in bold black type.

Declan read it and looked away.

"Mrs. Murray! Please! You *agreed*," Miss Everett said.

His mother retreated back to her corner. It was the first time Declan had ever seen that happen and he looked at Miss Everett with new respect.

"Do you understand why we are here, Declan?" Miss Everett asked, her voice calm again.

"Am I going to jail?"

"Do you think you should?"

He shrugged.

She glanced down at her notes. "Do you remember I told you about the Start 2 Project?"

He nodded and glanced at the video camera that stood on the tripod in the corner. It had been recording him during each of the daily assessment sessions he had had with Miss Everett. He knew she was assessing him for the social services department because she had told him so. She had also told him about the Start 2 Project, but he hadn't bothered to listen.

She glanced at her notes. "Truancy. Theft from a hardware store. Trespass on railway property. Graffiti and criminal damage. Maybe even arson. Not bad going for someone who has never been in trouble before," she said. "Is there anything else I should know?"

"I should have fried too," he said.

A long pause. He had their full attention and it made him feel good. Powerful. He had discovered his ability to shock with a few carefully chosen words while he was in the hospital.

"And why do you think that, Declan?" Miss Everett asked, unruffled. "Did *you* start the fire?"

He shook his head. "I told you, Jamal was smoking. It was an accident."

"Then why do you think you deserved to die?"

He shrugged. "Because the UXTs stick together."

"Yes, tell me about the Urban Xtreme Team," she said. "Jaz, Jamal, Tony, and B. J.—am I right?"

Declan closed his eyes and for a moment he could imagine Jaz standing there with his cap turned back to front. Messing around, joking with the others. They were all smiling, calling to him. Then the flames flickered up between them and he opened his eyes quickly.

"They were my friends," he said simply.

She checked her notes. "But you said yourself you hardly even knew them."

"So?"

"So why do you think they were your friends?"

He thought for a while then said, "Because they understood."

"I wish *I* did," his mother said.

Miss Everett ignored her. "Understood *what*, Declan?"

"What it's like. Life. Everything."

"*Life,*" she repeated the word and opened a buff folder on the desk in front of her and took out some pictures. He recognized them as his drawings. She leafed through them thoughtfully. "Your mother found these hidden under your bed and showed them to me."

"She had no right!"

"They are very good." She picked through them, pausing as she reached the picture of the boy with the butterfly wings pinned to the wall. "What makes you want to draw?"

"I don't know, I just do."

His mother could hold back no longer. "Why do you have to draw weird things like that? I just don't understand you. Gangs. Graffiti. Vandalism. It's all wrong!" she said. "I work twelve hours a day, six days a week to make sure you have everything. *Everything.* And you repay me with rubbish like this!" She snatched at the drawings and crumpled them up in front of his face.

"Maybe that's the problem," Miss Everett said carefully.

A sharp intake of breath. Then: "Oh, I see what you're saying!" she said. "Our son is out burning buildings and you blame his parents for not looking after him. Well, what are we supposed to do? Keep him locked up all day?"

Silence.

Miss Everett turned back to Declan. "A while ago," she said in a quiet voice, "someone just like you was sent to us for assessment. His name was Jason Rhodes and had been getting into trouble ever since his father was killed in a car wreck."

She shook her head sadly. "But we didn't have the funding for the Start 2 Project then and by the time we got it, it was too late."

Declan was listening. "What happened to him?"

"He spent some time in a penitentiary for young offenders and couldn't adjust to school when he came out," she said. "Oh, we tried to help him, but he wouldn't listen. That's why he ended up leading his friends up onto the roof of a burning building where they all died except one."

"You mean Jaz!"

She nodded. "I knew Jason wasn't bad as soon as I saw him. Not deep down bad, like some people. He had lost his dad. He was faced with a world he didn't understand and nobody seemed to care. He was frightened and the UXTs seemed to be his answer."

"You're lying—Jaz wasn't scared of anything."

"Not scared—*frightened*," Miss Everett corrected him. "He was and so were the others, and you too. We all are in one way or another, if only we would admit it. Some of us are frightened of failure." Declan saw his mother shift uncomfortably. "Others just want to stop the world for a moment so they can catch a breath." His dad's nod was bearly perceptible. "And some of us are frightened of facing it all alone."

Declan looked away.

Miss Everett tapped her papers into a pile. "*Life* sometimes sounds like a sentence," she said. "The Start 2 Project is designed to prove life is for living."

A loud knock and the door opened. Declan recognized the reporter's pale face immediately.

"Jerry Redback, the *Herald*," he announced, flashing his press ID card as if it excused his intrusion. "Just a few questions."

"You have no right barging in here!"

The man silenced Miss Everett's protests with a chopping motion of a hand covered in chunky rings. "I think my readers have *every* right to know what's going on here, Miss Everett," he said in a matter-of-fact voice. "You see, filth like him should be locked up, not mothered at the taxpayers' expense by a load of soft, do-gooders in the department of social services."

"Mr Redback! Please! You don't understand."

"Oh, I understand all right," he said. "I understand that kids nowadays think they can get away with anything." He thrust a blunt finger in Declan's face. "Well, you're wrong, kid. Dead wrong. And I'm going to make sure that when they lock you up they throw away the key as an example to the rest of your maggot kind."

Miss Everett's face was flushed an angry pink by the time he left. When she spoke, her voice had lost much of its usual calm.

"So there you have it, Declan," she said. "You can let me help or you can allow people like *him* to write you off. They'll say you're no good. They'll say it's a waste of time giving you a second chance. But I believe you're worth it. The question is, do you, Declan? It's up to you. You decide!"

7

The big four-wheel drive lurched, one wheel spinning on the edge of the road until it found traction in the snow. Big Foot changed down a gear, sending the note of the engine screaming up as they began to climb the next rise.

Declan held on as the Land Cruiser bounced about, praying the journey would end before the crazy old Indian sent them plunging into the ravine below.

The journey had started more quietly with Miss Everett in her red Ford, driving out of Vancouver on the Fraser Highway. They passed Charlie, Big Bird, and Sad Face, but he could not bring himself to look at them. So he watched the line of second-hand car lots slide by on the other side instead, their red-and-white bunting fluttering in the breeze. Miss Everett turned on to Highway 1 and suddenly they were free of the urban sprawl, leapfrogging the railway line as they followed the Fraser River east toward Hope.

"You will like Big Foot," Miss Everett promised as they passed the road sign to Hell's Gate and picked up the Coquihalla Highway. "He knows the mountains around Glacier National Park better than anyone."

"What kind of name is Big Foot?" Declan asked.

"Indian," she said. "His great grandfather was a famous chief."

Declan watched the reflection of the bridges in the windscreen and pretended not to listen as she told him about Moose Jaw Ski Lodge.

"You'll be staying with Big Foot and his wife Mary," she said. "Helping them out at Moose Jaw. It gets pretty busy at this time of year so there'll be plenty of work for you to do. But don't expect to be paid—you'll be working for your bed and board."

"Thought they had banned slavery," he muttered.

She ignored him. "And your mom and dad can come and visit you any time."

"Right, like she's really going to take time off work to do that," he said. "She said it cost her a bunch to pay the fine."

They drove in silence for a while before Miss Everett spoke.

"I know it has been tough for you, Declan," she said, "but I want you to remember that a lot of people are sticking their necks out to give you a second chance. So don't blow it. Because if you do, you'll find yourself back in front of that judge quicker than you can spit out your gum. Then there'll be nothing I can do to help you. Do you understand?"

He understood all right. Six weeks of slavery, stuck in the mountains in the middle of winter with an Indian teaching him the mysterious ways of his forefathers—and all for his own good! He was beginning to wish he hadn't volunteered for her Start 2 Project.

Big Foot was waiting for them at the town of

Kamloops as arranged. His beat-up Land Cruiser was parked in a service station by the side of a blue lake just outside of town.

Declan had imagined him tall, silent, wearing a full Indian headdress of eagle feathers that sprouted out of his head and trailed to the ground. He was disappointed.

Big Foot turned out to be a wiry, old man who looked more like Yoda than a great Indian chief. His face was cut by wrinkles and his bushy gray hair was tied back in a ponytail. He had bow legs and enormous hands that made his arms seem impossibly thin and spindly. And instead of eagle feathers, he was wearing old jeans and a dirty, sheepskin jacket with the sleeves cut off.

"Remember what I told you, Declan," Miss Everett said as she handed him his small black bag. "You've got to give it a chance."

He threw his bag onto the floor of the Land Cruiser and slid onto the tattered bench seat, then sat staring at the crack in the windscreen. He did not bother to look at her as they pulled away.

Declan soon discovered Big Foot wasn't a silent, mystical type of person. In fact, the old man was quite the opposite. Talking incessantly as he drove, clicking his tongue and chuckling to himself as he told Declan about the last year's run of sockeye salmon on the rivers of the national park. It didn't seem important to him that Declan wasn't interested. He just kept on talking, raising dust from his jeans as he slapped his spindly thigh, grinning every time he mentioned bears:

"Nine feet tall on their hind legs, some of them," he said, clearly impressed. "Brown bears all lined up in the water to catch the leaping salmon as they jump the rapids. That is a sight you must see, my young friend!"

The way the old man was driving, Declan was beginning to wonder if he would see anything ever again.

They screeched off the main road before they reached Kicking Horse Pass and followed the signs for Timberwolf. Twisting through the conifers and winter pines as the mountains grew steadily around them, their snowy peaks poking out through the dark green of the forests that blanketed the slopes.

Soon the road had narrowed into a single track between two high banks of snow, but Big Foot did not slow down. Declan began to feel breathless, and light-headed, and sick.

"The mountain air is thinner. It makes you dizzy," Big Foot shouted over the roar of the engine, never considering that Declan's discomfort might have something to do with the way he was driving.

Then, at last, they skidded around a bend and Declan caught his first glimpse of Timberwolf Mountain. Rising up in front of them forever. Jagged against the sky. Three points of rock each higher than the next with a plume of snow, like a white standard fluttering in the wind, blowing off the topmost. A glacier shimmered in the sunlight, a teardrop of ice running down one side of its face, to end by a frozen lake where the town nestled among the trees.

And yet, for all its breathless beauty, the mountain left Declan feeling strangely cold. He shivered and looked away. Only to find his eyes drawn irresistibly back up to the peak.

Big Foot just smiled and said nothing.

The Land Cruiser scattered the shoppers in the main street, hurtled past the wooden fronted shops and hotels without slowing down once, then shot out the other side.

"Welcome to Moose Jaw, my young friend," he said as they screeched to a halt outside a small ski lodge set apart from the rest. A sign on the gate said: BEST COOKING IN TOWN.

"You're crazy!" Declan said, as he wrenched open the door and jumped out just in case Big Foot decided to take off again.

It was still early, but the sun was already disappearing behind the mountains to the west, its dying rays gilding the icicles that bearded the eves of the roof and made the snow lumpy with shadow. A wisp of smoke curled lazily from the chimney into the still air and the windows glowed with a warm light.

"Better get inside," Big Foot said, looking up at the cloudless blue sky. "Blizzard's coming."

8

Midnight, and Declan was ready to leave.

He had been lying awake in the darkness for hours. Fully dressed. Bag still packed. Listening to the wind whistling around the window of his tiny attic bedroom.

Gradually, the noises downstairs had faded as the paying guests had gone to bed. Still he waited.

Nothing was going to stop him now. He was heading south. Across the border into Washington. Then California. He would go to Hollywood, get a job with a film studio, and become a big star and a friend of Judge Dredd.

Maybe then they'll leave me alone, he decided as he slipped from under the covers and picked up his bag.

The door came open with a loud click. He froze, listening. Only the steady tick of a clock. He moved on down the steep stairs toward the light and the passage below.

His footsteps whispered to the patterns on the carpet as he crept past the numbered rooms and turned down the main stairs toward the reception desk. From there he had a clear run to the front door.

He reached the bottom of the stairs and looked back, sure someone was following him. Watching him. Waiting to see what he would do. But he decided it must have been the shadows tricking his eyes and filling his head with half-seen movement. Still, the fine hairs on the nape of his neck prickled his skin and he shivered.

"This place is beginning to freak me out," he murmured.

To his surprise, Declan found the front door unlocked, but he soon realized it might just as well have been barred and bolted. When he opened it, he found the world outside had changed. What had been a calm, blue evening had become a swirling, whirling mass of snow. Giant flakes driven by the wind. Creating patterns that formed in the light from the open door, then disappeared again just as quickly, shredded by ferocious gusts of arctic air.

He shouldered the door closed again, leaned back against it, and closed his eyes as he fought his rising feeling of panic. Wild thoughts of being trapped sent his head into a spin. Declan forced himself to stay calm and think. The storm could not last forever. So he sat down on his bag and settled against the wall to wait for the blizzard to blow itself out.

He stared at the brightly painted eagles in the picture on the wall opposite and listened to the slow ticking of the clock. And gradually Declan began to drift. Floating up to join the eagles as, one by one, they spread their wings and lifted off their mountain aeries, wheeling higher and higher into the sky beneath the starburst of a yellow-ocher sun.

Jaz burst up out of the fire. Screaming. His body was covered in flaming feathers. His eyes were burning red coals. Like some awesome, living totem, he spread his phoenix wings to fly, only to crumble away to dust, his ashes scattering on the wind, lost forever.

"Jaz!" Declan shouted himself awake.

He blinked at the wrinkled, old face in front of him and wondered if he was still dreaming.

Big Foot's thoughtful expression changed and he grinned a gap-toothed smile. "It's good to see you up so early, my friend," he said. "There's always plenty of work to be done here."

Declan realized he was still sitting on his bag by the front door and groaned. He had let the night slip away without him.

Big Foot patted his shoulder. "Come," he said, without appearing to notice the bag. "You have much to learn."

"About the ways of your forefathers, I s'pose."

Big Foot looked puzzled. "About serving coffee and waffles, my young friend," he said and went striding away down the hall. The smell of frying eggs belched out as the door swung closed behind him.

Declan did not hesitate. He grabbed his bag and threw open the door, but all thoughts of escape vanished when he looked out. It was still snowing hard and the dawn's creeping light was yellow and sickly. Nothing much existed beyond

the Land Cruiser parked outside. Even Timberwolf Mountain had been swallowed up, leaving
only the feeling of its presence to haunt his sixth
sense.

He had little choice but to close the door and
resign himself to spending one more day with Big
Foot and Mary.

"How did you know—about the storm, I
mean?" he asked Big Foot as they sat at the
kitchen table, eating breakfast.

Big Foot smeared the egg yolk from his chin
with the back of his hand. "Old Indian trick."

"More like, watching the weather forecast,"
Mary said, winking at Declan.

No matter how hard he tried, he couldn't help
liking Mary. She was small, gray-haired and neat,
and had the sort of eyes that always seemed to
find something to smile about.

Big Foot washed his last, copious mouthful
down with a mug of scalding black coffee.
Burped loudly. Muttered something about light-
ing the fire in the dining room before the guests
came down for breakfast, and stood up scratch-
ing his chest. He told Declan to follow.

"First you set the tables for breakfast," Big
Foot said. "Then you serve the coffee when the
guests come down. And remember, they are on
vacation—you are not."

So Declan stifled his yawns and served the coffee, listening to the skiers as they discussed the
bad weather over waffles spread thick with maple
syrup.

"Big Foot reckons the weather has closed in for

at least forty-eight hours," the man at Table 1 said.

Table 5 nodded. "Should be some mighty fine powder when it blows itself out."

"And avalanches," Brown Beard at Table 3 said gloomily. "Last year they cut the main road. Couldn't get down the mountain for a week."

Startled, Declan knocked an open jar of maple syrup into his lap.

"Stupid kid! Look what you've done!" Brown Beard said, jumping up. "That's a two-thousand-dollar ski suit you've ruined."

"I didn't mean to!"

All eyes were on him. Staring. Hostile. Declan brandished the pot of boiling coffee at them like a sword.

"The kid's wacko!" Brown Beard told Mary as she came hurrying out of the kitchen to see what all the noise was about.

"Steady, Declan," she soothed. "We all know it was an accident."

Declan dropped the pot—SMASH—turned, dodged around Table 5, and fled into the hall. His bag was in his hand in a moment. He threw open the front door with a crash that nearly had it off its hinges and brought a small avalanche of snow down from the roof just as he stepped outside. It buried him with a soft FLUMPFF!

He came up gasping and started dancing about, wriggling as the snow melted and trickled down his neck in icy trails.

"It makes my heart warm to see you do that, my young friend," Big Foot said, appearing out of the snow suddenly. His arms were full of chopped firewood, but Declan had the feeling he had been standing out there for some time.

"What d'ya mean!" Declan snarled.

The old man nodded his approval. "Exercises will help you to keep fit," he said. "And you will need all your strength if you are to face the Great Wolf."

9

"No one said anything about a wolf!"

"You did not ask."

"And how was I supposed to know?"

Big Foot did not reply, just kept stacking wood.

Declan decided he would take his chances back in the city—like Jaz had—and nothing anyone could say was going to change his mind.

"Why should I care if you leave?" the old man said. "No one is forcing you to stay."

"You're not going to try and stop me?"

Big Foot shook his head. "It is up to you, my young friend," he said, "but I do not think you will go far with all the roads blocked. Unless . . ."

He left the word hanging.

Declan waited for it to drop, but it didn't. "Unless? Unless what?" he asked, frustrated.

"Unless you can ski or use a snowboard," Big Foot said. "Then perhaps I could guide you down the mountain." He paused from his labors with the wood and studied Declan's face for a moment, then shook his head as if he had made up his mind about something important. "But I cannot teach *you.*"

The way he said it made Declan angry. "Why not? What's wrong with me?"

"It is simple," Big Foot said. "How can I teach someone who is not going to be here?"

Declan hopped from foot to foot as he looked around. If anything the weather was closing in. The wind was rising, driving the snow into his face and hands, until his cheeks were stinging and his fingers numb. He remembered what Brown Beard had said about avalanches cutting the road.

"S'posing I do stay until the storm blows out," he said, "how long would it take to teach me to use a snowboard?"

"Not long—if you have the heart to learn."

Declan made up his mind. "OK—I'll stay, but I'm not going anywhere near any wolves!"

"A wise decision for one so young," Big Foot said, dumping the last of the wood on the pile as if it had suddenly lost all importance. "And since you have decided to stay, we will start your training right away."

Declan soon discovered the old man could move with surprising speed. He had to run fast to keep up as they jogged into town. Chasing Big Foot's misty shadow through the swirling snow. Tracing his footsteps before the prints disappeared. Wondering all the while if wolves were ever hungry enough to come right into town.

Big Foot stopped at a shop in the main street called "The Snow Shack." He paused before opening the door.

"I have told no one of your reasons for coming to Timberwolf, only that you are here to learn," he said. "One day perhaps you will feel strong enough to tell them the truth. Who knows? Until then we will leave things the way they are."

No chance of that happening, Declan thought as he followed the old man inside.

The sudden warmth made the skin on Declan's face and fingers tingle. The wooden walls were lined with racks of skis and ski poles; some for sale, most for rent. Clothes hung on chrome rods and the light glinted on the polished toes of the ski boots. But the snowboards caught his eye most of all.

He had only seen them in magazines and the freestyle boards were much bigger than the skateboards he was used to. Curling up at the nose and tail and covered in motifs and logos. No wheels underneath, of course. Only adjustable bindings on the flat center for the snowboarder's feet.

One board in particular stood out from the rest. Glossy black. Its glassy surface still shiny and smooth—unlike the other boards that had been scratched through constant use—and a mythical bird of prey painted in bright colors on the underside.

He reached out and touched the horns on the bird's head, then ran his fingers down its hooked beak and along the zigzags of lightning fire that came shooting out of its eyes.

"It's a Thunderbird," a voice said suddenly.

He pulled his hand away as if he had touched something electric and looked around. A girl was standing beside him.

"Indian legends say it makes the lightning with a blink of its eye and the thunder when it flaps its wings," she said and smiled. "Pretty awesome bird, don't you think?"

Declan opened his mouth to agree, but no sound came out so he closed it again quickly.

"This is Emmanuelle," Big Foot said, introducing them. "She is the daughter of my friend Alain Jonquiere—the owner."

Declan could see a short man with a tanned face and a fat mustache through the door, stacking boxes in the storeroom at the back.

"Everyone calls me Manu," she said, her accent was light but unmistakably French.

"Nanu that's mice," Declan said, then, realizing what he had said, felt stupid. Things weren't going too well.

She laughed and tucked her long, dark hair behind an ear that glinted with a crescent of silver earrings. At first glance, her mouth had seemed a little too wide for her face, but her smile fixed all that.

Declan realized he was staring and looked away quickly.

"My young friend is from the city," Big Foot said. "But he does not want to stay with us long."

Manu's dark eyes shot daggers of light. "Timberwolf too quiet for you?"

"It's not that, it's just," Declan started to explain, then changed his mind and turned back to the snowboard.

A pause.

"If you haven't ridden a Thunderbird down a mountain then you haven't lived," she said.

Declan glanced at Big Foot suspiciously. "Do you think he really knows how to use one of these?" he asked Manu in a whisper.

"He should," Manu said and laughed. "He's only the best instructor in Timberwolf—he can teach anyone anything."

Strangely, that wizened old man seemed to have grown taller since breakfast.

Big Foot asked Manu to pick out all the snowboarding equipment Declan would need and went through to haggle with her father who, he said, owed him a favor or two. Free rental for as long as he wanted the equipment seemed to be the acceptable price the grandson of a great chief would pay.

"Is he for real?" Declan asked when Big Foot had gone.

"That depends."

"On what?"

"On whether you want him to be."

"But he's weird—and what's all this stuff about a wolf?"

Her mouth fitted neatly into her smile. "He means the mountain—Timberwolf Mountain," she said. "He calls it that because of Numuna."

"Num-who-a?"

"It means Gray Wolf. A great spirit the legends say lives in these mountains. A wolf which is supposed to have created all the people and the whole universe way back at the beginning of time. They say it howls when something bad is going to happen on the mountain—people have heard it."

"That's stupid," Declan scoffed. "How could a wolf do all that?"

She didn't reply, just arched her back angrily

and busied herself with the bindings on the board. The silence left Declan feeling awkward and uneasy.

He watched as she carefully adjusted the bindings on the flat of the board so they were just the right distance apart to fit his stance.

"Are you French?" he asked, deciding to change the subject.

"French Canadian," she answered, picking out a pair of soft boots for him. She relaxed a little. "We moved here from Quebec when Papa opened the shop."

The boots looked a bit like high-top basketball shoes, purple-black with a white Mass-A-Tak logo flashing on the side. She showed him how to lace them up correctly and made him flex his ankles. They were supple enough to move easily and still hold his heel firmly in place. A perfect fit in the bindings.

"And you? No school?" she asked, turning her attention to clothes.

"Me?" Declan had to think quickly.

His mind raced as she picked out a Silver Zag half-baggie jacket and snowboard trousers with reinforced patches on the knees. A cap, goggles, and gloves for cold weather. And finally a small black case. She seemed surprised to find the sunglasses were missing from inside and had to try another before she found a pair for Declan.

"You don't have to tell me," she said, as he tried on the sunglasses, "not if you don't want to."

"I do!" he blurted, glad the sunglasses masked his eyes. "It's just that, I'm on extended leave," he said eventually. "I've been—sick."

A lie seemed so much easier at the time. How could he tell someone like her the truth? About Jaz, Jamal, Tony, and B. J.? About the fire?

"So you have come to the mountains to get well?" she asked.

"Sort of," he said, beginning to feel uncomfortable again.

Three days passed before Declan saw Manu again. Three days, four hours, and almost thirty-five minutes, but he definitely wasn't counting. And all the while, Big Foot seemed intent on making his life total misery.

Early morning:

"You're late," the old man said, poking at him with a bony finger.

Declan squinted through the crack in his eyelids. The clock by his bedside said 5:05 a.m.

"More like SOS," he groaned.

Big Foot made him set the tables and chop the firewood, then together they jogged a couple of miles around the town in the snow before breakfast. Declan had the weirdest feeling he was trapped inside a huge snow globe—stuck on a mantelpiece somewhere to be shaken up for some giant's amusement—and that he would never escape Big Foot's constant coaxing and cajoling. So by the time they reached Moose Jaw again, he was cold and tired and wet. "And just in time to serve breakfast to our guests," Big Foot said, grinning happily.

Dark thoughts filled Declan's head.

Only the knowledge that his misery would soon end sustained him through the worst of that first terrible day on the beginner's slope. Exercises first. Waddling around with his left foot strapped into the binding on the snowboard, his right foot free, feeling awkward and stupid as the board flapped about like a big, unwieldy foot.

"You must grow used to the board. Let it become part of you," Big Foot explained, showing him the correct stance. "Relax your upper body. Hands forward. Knees bent. I said, knees *bent!*"

The lesson went on all day. A crash course with Declan doing all the crashing as he struggled to master the use of the edge on the slope. Heel edge. Toe edge. Forward. Backward. Trying to keep his weight over the center of the board, like Big Foot said. Pushing down with his hips, using his body weight as he slid down the slope in step turns.

As the night closed in, he trudged back, carrying his snowboard on his back as if it was a cross he had to bear. With only a long evening of waiting on tables and washing up dishes to look forward to. Then falling into bed, only to be shaken awake in what seemed like moments.

"And you're late again, my young friend."

Declan buried his face in the pillow. "I'm *not* your stinking friend!" he screamed, voice muffled.

The second day began with a fall from the drag lift. The metal button-seat escaping him, twanging away on its spring, leaving him helplessly slithering back down the steep slope to end up in a heap at the bottom by the lift operator's hut.

"You must like the taste of snow, my young friend," Big Foot said, slapping his thigh and chuckling to himself.

Gradually, however, as the day drifted toward afternoon, Declan's confidence began to grow.

Big Foot noticed the change immediately. "That's it!" he said, clapping his gloved hands. "Stop fighting the board and feel the energy of the slope beneath. Let it flow through you. Let it become part of you."

Declan relaxed and immediately his turns became smoother. The day wore on into the afternoon and he began to establish a rhythm. Soon he was sweeping in curves across the fall line. Leaving garland patterns in the snow as he linked each turn to the next, crisscrossing the slope in easy traverses.

So by the morning of the third day, he was confidently pointing the curling nose of his board down any slope presented to him. Bending at the knees to lower his center of gravity, rolling his ankles to shift his weight from heel edge to toe in a series of linked turns that impressed even Big Foot.

"I have taught you well, my young friend," he said, looking pleased with himself, "but you still have more to learn."

"You could teach me that too," Declan said.

But Big Foot shook his head and looked up at the sky.

Declan pushed his goggles up onto his forehead. For the first time, he noticed it had almost stopped snowing. The wind had dropped, too, and patches of blue were appearing as the clouds tore themselves away from the peaks of the mountain to drift away to the north.

"The storm has passed, my young friend," Big Foot said, solemnly. "The road down the mountain will soon be open. If you still wish to leave Timberwolf, then the time has come."

Declan hardly touched the free sandwiches Big Foot wangled from the waitress at the Spotted Walrus Café. Instead, he just sat in a sunless corner, kicking splinters off the leg of the table and trying to ignore the chatter and laughter of the happy people around him.

The slopes of Timberwolf Mountain had come alive after the storm. Skiers and snowboarders wearing bright suits and smiles emerged with the sunshine. Calling and waving to one another as they stepped off the cable cars. Hurrying to catch the chairlifts farther up the mountain where the fresh powder had been dumped in heaps by the storm.

He watched them over the ragged line of skis that had grown up around the Spotted Walrus as people stopped for something to eat. Planting the ends of their skis in the snow, points up, to form a rickety fence. He wanted to kick it down. Smash through. So he could be free and happy like the people on the other side.

Big Foot chewed through his sandwich, swallowed hard, and eyed the one in front of Declan hungrily. "No point in wasting it," he said, when he could bear it no longer.

Declan looked away, wishing he could strap on his board and escape. He longed to just fly down the slopes.

"What if I've changed my mind?" he asked, after a long pause, "about going back to Vancouver, I mean."

Big Foot stopped chasing mayonnaise around his fingers with his long pink tongue and stared thoughtfully at him for a while, then shook his head. "It is better that you go," he said. "You might change your mind again and steal away like a thief in the night."

"No way! I would never do that—I swear."

Big Foot smiled sadly as if he had set some test and Declan had just failed it miserably.

Only then did Declan realize what he had said and felt the blood hot in his face. "You knew all along, didn't you? You *were* following me that night."

Big Foot did not answer, just stuffed the rest of the sandwich in his mouth and chewed through it determinedly.

"Please!" Declan begged. "You've got to give me a second chance."

"It seems you need many of these *second chances*, my young friend," Big Foot said, punctuating the words with pieces of chewed-up lettuce. "And anyway, soon I will be taking Manu and the others up the mountain. You would only get in the way."

"You're taking Manu up the mountain? Why?"

Declan glanced up at the three jagged peaks. He shivered. The mountain still made his skin crawl. He couldn't explain why. He knew only that it had some strange hold over him as if he was tied to it by invisible threads. Somehow, somewhere up among those towering peaks, lay his future. His life. Maybe even his death.

Big Foot smoothed his wrinkled face and took his time to explain. "I know it is hard for you to believe, but I am getting old," he said. "If the truth be known, I grow weary. Sometimes the cold makes my bones ache. I know soon I will journey up the mountain for the last time." He glanced lovingly at the mountain. "So I must teach others the secret ways of the Great Wolf."

"Secret ways? You mean like hidden trails?"

"The mountain holds many secrets," the old man said, mysteriously. "I must pass on the knowledge I have gained in my lifetime to others so the secrets will not be forgotten. Manu already understands much about the ways of the Great Wolf and she, like Noah and perhaps even the one they call Mad Dog, can do much to teach the ones who come here to respect the beauty of this place."

Declan studied the plume of snow blowing off the top peak and wondered, not for the first time, why it was that others could see the beauty of the mountain while he could only be haunted by it.

"It takes strength and courage to face the unknown," Big Foot said, as if he could read the thoughts in Declan's head. "Up there, the Great Wolf is always ready to test our weaknesses and prove our strengths. To understand the mountain, we must first understand ourselves. So the journey is one of understanding as much as it is a challenge and I do not believe *you* are ready for such a journey yet."

Declan shifted uncomfortably, but Big Foot held his gaze, staring deep into his eyes as if they were little windows and he was searching for something inside. Big Foot was still considering what he saw there when the news of the avalanche reached them.

Declan saw Manu first. She was moving fast, cutting down the slope. A flash of color, like a darting blue jay in the dappled sunlight threading through the trees. She reached the Spotted Walrus and slid to a halt, carving a wave in the snow.

"It looked bad," she said to Big Foot breathlessly. "Noah and I were up on Snowdance Trail, we saw a helicopter dropping skiers off on the peak, three of them came straight down from Timberwolf Top." She caught her breath. "We saw them on the glacier and thought they were going to climb up to the Refuge, but they cut across and took the drop on the Wolf instead."

"They chose the trail of the Howling Wolf?" Big Foot was startled.

Manu nodded. "We saw the cornice give way as they went over the edge. It looked like the whole mountain was moving. They were swallowed by the Wolf—that's for sure," she said. "Noah is already up there with the rescue team."

Big Foot's face set grimly. "This is what happens when people do not show respect for the mountain," he said. "You have done well to find me. Mountain Rescue will need help so I must ask you to look after my young friend here. Make sure he gets back to Moose Jaw. He soon has a long journey to make."

And with that he was gone.

"You're leaving?"

"I don't want to, not any more."

Manu looked puzzled. "But I thought..."

"I changed my mind," Declan said, quickly. "But it looks like I'm going to have to go unless I can prove to Big Foot I really want to stay."

"And how are you going to do that?"

Declan shrugged. "Don't know yet, but I'll think of something."

Manu strapped on her board and looked down the slope in front of them. "Race you to the pipe!"

Without waiting, she pointed the nose of her board down the slope and left him sitting, fumbling with the clip on his leash. He pushed his feet into the bindings, but forgot to edge the board across the slope and it slipped away from under him as he tried to stand up.

By the time the snow was crackling under his board, she had already reached the bottom of the slope. The breeze dusted the snow in fine showers from the dark pine trees around her as she stood easily on her board and watched his descent.

"Not bad," she said, as he carved into a turn and stopped.

"Done a bit of skateboarding," he said, trying to sound as laid-back as possible. He overdid it and fell over backward.

She laughed. "Grommit!"

And she was right. He was *just* a beginner. One look at the action on the halfpipe told him that.

Snowboarders were going off in a steady stream. Carving lines between the walls of snow that banked up on either side like two parallel waves in a frozen sea. Blasting off the lip. Tumbling like acrobats in the air. Snowboards making semaphore of the sunlight. Landing easily to head for the lip on the other side. Zigzagging down the steep slope, each trying to out-perform the one who had gone before.

Declan noticed the way she was watching one in particular.

"That's Carl Martin," Manu said. "Everyone calls him Mad Dog Martin because there's nothing he won't do. He's sixteen and some people say he's already good enough for the Olympics."

Mad Dog hit the lip and took off in a snow-burst that starred the sky like a pure white firework. He turned a full 360 degrees in the air and landed perfectly.

"How did he get that good?" Declan asked, enviously.

"A lot of time. A lot of practice. And the right equipment."

"He's rich then," Declan concluded.

Manu shook her head, frowning as if a thought

had just occurred to her. "He's given up school to turn pro, but can't get a sponsor until he wins a big competition. He seems to do OK, though. Working odd jobs for people—even helps Papa in the shop on weekends."

They watched Mad Dog as he caught the lift, back up to the top of the pipe. Relaxed and easy. Eyes wrapped in sunglasses. His straggling red hair greasing the shoulders of his No Fear jacket. He spotted Manu and came cruising over, back foot out of the binding and resting casually on the flat of the board.

"Did you see me, girl?" he said. "I was *huge*, no sweat. Wiped them all. Figure I'll win the Pipe-Burner Comp for sure. No one round here can touch me."

"Carl isn't always as modest as this," Manu giggled.

"No point hiding it if you've got it," Mad Dog said, looking Declan up and down.

He noticed Declan's boots and whispered something in Manu's ear that Declan couldn't quite hear but which made her shift uncomfortably.

"Declan's from the city," she said, changing the subject.

"The smoke, huh? Just like I thought," Carl said. "All the right gear, but never hucked a twister off a kicker in your whole life."

"He's pretty good, if you must know," Manu said, sounding irritated. "You want to watch it— with a bit of practice he might even be able to beat you."

Mad Dog's eyes narrowed. "Is that so, well excuse me for not shivering in my sads." He turned to Declan. "Hey, bud—you ever been down the gurgler before?"

"I didn't mean Declan was ready for the halfpipe yet," Manu said, quickly. "And I promised Big Foot I would make sure he got back to Moose Jaw OK."

"What are you his babysitter too?"

Declan studied the line up. He watched a big kid ally oop off the lip.

"Suppose I could do that," he said, deciding it couldn't be too different from making the same jump on a skateboard.

Mad Dog grinned. "See the geek *wants* to kill himself!"

From the top, however, the halfpipe looked much steeper than it had from a distance. Much steeper and not nearly so wide. The walls rising up on either side into giant buttresses of hard-packed snow. He waited his turn in the line, trying to ignore his board, which had begun to feel like a big, unwieldy foot again.

"Why don't you just forget it?" Manu said, sounding nervous. "I mean, what am I going to tell Big Foot if you go and break your neck?"

Declan glanced at Mad Dog. He recognized that crazy look in his eyes. Declan felt the burning resentment. He had seen the same suspicion in other people and he knew this was about much more than just making a few jumps on a snowboard. And all the while the voice in his head was whispering.

"So do it!" Mad Dog said, as Declan reached the front of the line.

The halfpipe opened wide before him.

He shifted his weight, pulling the nose of his board around in line with the slope, and felt it come alive beneath his feet. By the time he had tapped into the groove worn in the snow by the snowboards that had gone down before, he was already going too fast.

The wall of snow raced up with frightening speed and stole his stomach as it threw him up toward the lip. He blasted off the top in a squall of snow. Instinctively, he reached down and grabbed the edge of his board and looked over his shoulder at the ground as it receded. The twisting motion sent him into a 180-degree turn, he lost momentum, and his weight began to drag him down.

Moments later, his board was thumping into the snow and running up the wall on the other side. He banged off the top again, somersaulted dangerously out of control, realized the board was where his head should have been, and just managed to pull it back under him before he hit the ground.

For the briefest of moments he felt electric. Unstoppable. Until the board caught an edge and tripped him, throwing him forward. He went down hard. Skittering across the slippery slope with the icy snow rubbing his face like sandpaper, tearing off his goggles and filling the neck of his jacket until the zipper burst.

He rolled onto his back and stared up at the

blue sky until Mad Dog's grinning face appeared upside down above him.

"Nice try, sucker, but you'll always be a loser," he said. "I'll see you *later!*"

Later! Later! Later! The word echoed inside Declan's throbbing head, as much a threat as a promise.

11

Saturday morning and Declan was up even earlier than usual. He crept downstairs accompanied only by the steady tick of the clock as Moose Jaw slumbered around him. But he wasn't running this time. In fact, he was determined to stay.

First, he chopped the wood and stacked the splintered pieces neatly by the fire. Then he set the tables, smoothing out the bright tablecloths and placing the silverware like pieces of a puzzle, ready for the guests to use. When everything was just right, he scrubbed and cleaned the kitchen and had it all ready for Mary and Big Foot when they came down.

"It's a pity others don't work as hard around here," Mary said, sending a meaningful glance in Big Foot's direction as she heaped a reward of waffles on Declan's plate.

Big Foot was waving his fork about with a piece of ham spiked on the prongs, retelling the story of how he had—singlehandedly—found the three skiers trapped by the avalanche just by sense of smell.

"I smell better than a dog," he said, cramming the ham into his mouth and washing it down with swigs of coffee.

"You eat like one, too," Mary complained.

Big Foot said nothing about taking him back

to Vancouver, so Declan finished his breakfast quickly and surprised them by volunteering to wash the dishes. And later, when the guests came down, he helped at the tables willingly, without yawning or complaining once, even earning a tip from Brown Beard on Table 3.

"I will look after that for you," Big Foot said, holding out his hand.

Declan caressed the five-dollar bill longingly, then handed it over. Big Foot grinned and plucked it from his fingers. Declan bit his lip— sorely tested—and said nothing as he watched it disappear into the depths of the old man's coat.

"Will you teach me some jumps on the half-pipe?" Declan asked, when at last all the work was done.

Big Foot shook his head. "I am too old a dog for new tricks."

Declan was disappointed. "Well, how am I supposed to learn if you won't teach me?"

"I said *I* am too old for new tricks," Big Foot said, smiling. "Perhaps, if you asked Manu . . ."

"You mean it?"

Big Foot nodded, but his smile faded and he became stern.

"But remember, you will live to regret it if I have to come looking for you, my headstrong friend," he said. "So be sure to return long before the sun dips behind the mountain!"

Declan did not hesitate. He stamped his feet into his Mass-A-Taks, picked up his board on the way out, and was gone before Big Foot could change his mind.

It was still early and the morning mist lingered, trailing like torn wool caught on the branches of the dark pine trees on the slopes above the town. His breath steamed on air so crisp it prickled the membranes of his nose like pins and smelled as clean and shiny as polished metal.

He glanced up at the mountain as the first rays of the sun flicked over its shoulder and set fire to a million points on the frosted roofs. He still felt its towering weight and his skin began to creep but, for the first time since he had arrived in Timberwolf, he did not look away.

He forced his gaze along the razor edge of the ridge, then down the steep embankment to the glacier, and finally let it climb to the top peak itself. And slowly an idea took shape like a picture in his mind. An idea that left him feeling dizzy and lightheaded.

He was just going over his plan in his mind when he turned the corner to the main street and almost bumped into Mad Dog.

Mad Dog had his face pressed against the window of The Snow Shack and was peering inside as if he was looking for someone he didn't want to see. Declan ducked back around the corner and watched him.

Mad Dog glanced up and down the street. Most of the shops were still closed so few people were about. He reached around his neck and tugged at a piece of string until a key popped out, glinting as it dangled in the sunlight. It fit the lock and the shop bell tinkled as he opened the door and slipped inside.

Declan moved on down the street quickly and looked in the window. It was dark inside and a sign on the door said *Closed*. He picked out a shadow moving about among the carousels of clothing and watched it slide over to the counter by the till. Eventually it dissolved into the deeper shadows at the back of the shop.

Declan tried the door. It moved gently to his touch. He pushed it open a little way and hovered on the threshold, listening to the faint scrabbling noises coming from the storeroom. The voice in his head told him to leave it. Mad Dog was someone else's problem, it said.

He let the door swing closed and stepped back into the street. It was too risky to get involved, he decided, especially with his record. He turned and was about to walk away when he remembered Manu.

He swore under his breath. I must be crazy, he thought, looking around for help.

One glance over his shoulder at the empty street behind told him he was on his own. It would take too long to go for help. Mad Dog would have left by the time he returned. Who would believe him then—without proof?

He flattened his back against the frame of the door until it hurt and just managed to wriggle inside without jangling the bell. The air stirred through the shadows as he let the door swing shut behind him. Heart thumping and breathless, he stood while his eyes grew accustomed to the half-light. A step. Pause. Another step. It took all his stealth to move to the counter.

Beyond, the storeroom was a jumble of dark and light. The light coming through the half-open door that led out into the yard at the back. The dark wrapping the room in shades of gray edged in velvet black.

Mad Dog was over by the table. An empty cardboard box lay open in front of him. Declan watched as he carefully replaced the lid, then moved out of the light and his line of sight. Moments later, he returned empty-handed and stuffed something lumpy into a large plastic sack. He tied the neck of the sack, dragged it to the door and out into the yard where he left it by the wall with some others.

The sound of the shop bell. A flick of a switch. Instantly, the shadows around him vanished and he was left blinking in the glare of the spotlights.

"What are you doing in 'ere?" Monsieur Jonquiere asked, his mustache rising like hackles when he saw Declan.

"It's Mad Dog!" Declan said, pointing toward the storeroom. "In there. We can still catch him if we're quick."

"Wait just one minute!"

"But he's getting away."

Monsieur Jonquiere called out and the sound of his voice brought Mad Dog running. He was surprised to see Declan. "What's going on Mr. J?"

"That is what I am trying to find out. I found this young man sneaking around in the dark. Then 'e tells me it's because 'e saw you breaking in."

"And why would I want to do that?" Mad Dog asked, pulling at the string around his neck. He dangled the key in front of Declan's nose.

Declan stared at it as it turned slowly, twisting on the string. "But you didn't turn on the lights," he said. "And what's in that plastic sack?"

The smug look disappeared from Mad Dog's face and his eyes narrowed into a glare. "You shouldn't go spying on people, drongo! Not if you know what's good for you," he said, then remembered Manu's father and shrugged. "Trash."

Declan frowned. "Trash?"

"Yeah, you know—*garbage*. The stuff most people put in plastic sacks and leave out in yards. I'm meant to put it out first thing in the morning, right Mr. J?"

Declan went cold as he watched Manu's father nod his head.

Hadn't Manu mentioned something about Mad Dog helping out in her father's shop on weekends? Yes. Now he came to think about it, she had.

"Which explains why Carl is 'ere," Monsieur Jonquiere said, "but not *you*."

"I came to see Manu!" Declan tried to explain. "I saw Mad Dog at the window. I thought . . . ," he shrugged. "I don't know what I thought." The words turned to dust on his tongue and finally dried up altogether.

"A lot of valuable stock 'as been disappearing recently," Manu's father said. "I should call the police."

"The cops!" Declan began to panic.

"Sounds guilty to me, Mr. J." Mad Dog was

quick to agree. He gave Declan a sly look, as if he recognized something they had in common. Some dark secret that set them both apart.

Declan watched Manu's father move away from the door toward the counter and reach determinedly for the telephone. His head was spinning now. Wild thoughts tumbled in a confusing whirl, mixing him up and blinding his mind's eye. The door was open. It wasn't far. A few yards, no more. He could make a break for it. Easy. NO! Well, maybe he should take his chances outside. Run. "And don't stop for no one," Jaz's voice came back to him.

He was saved by the bell. The shop bell.

"Papa?" Manu stood looking quizzical in the doorway. Her smile faded, leaving her mouth set and awkward. "What's going on?"

"Mr. J caught your little friend with his stickies in the cash register," Mad Dog said, grinning.

"That's not true!" Declan snarled, cornered. He turned to Manu. "I only came to ask if you would teach me some tricks on the halfpipe."

"Yeah, right!" Mad Dog said sarcastically.

"I am calling the police," Monsieur Jonquiere persisted, waving the telephone.

"Wait, Papa!" Manu said, wanting to know precisely what had happened. She listened carefully and looked at Mad Dog suspiciously when Declan reached the part about the empty cardboard box. "I know *Declan* wouldn't steal anything, Papa," she said at last.

Her father was not so sure. The blood squeaked in Declan's ears as he waited for him to make up his mind. In the end, however, Monsieur Jonquiere grunted and put down the telephone.

"Well, if you say so, Manu," he said, still sounding doubtful, "but something strange is going on around 'ere, that is for sure."

Mad Dog glowered angrily at Declan, then noticed Manu's accusing look and suddenly decided he had a lot to do in the storeroom.

Later, when Declan and Manu reached the halfpipe, he stopped and looked at her. He tried to find the right words, but all he could come up with was, "Thanks."

"What for?"

"For . . . trusting me, I guess."

She smiled. "I know you wouldn't lie to me, Declan."

He laughed, but it sounded weak and awkward. "No way," he said, beginning to feel very uncomfortable again.

12

That evening the weather closed in again. The wind swung unexpectedly into the north, bringing heavy gray clouds with it. The clouds wrapped themselves around the peaks of Timberwolf Mountain and spilled down the glacier, sending squally snow showers sweeping down the valley in a confusion of flakes.

The bad weather lasted almost two weeks, but Declan hardly noticed. He spent every moment of his spare time on the halfpipe or on the kicker nearby. He practiced hard. Nothing radical at first, but gradually his confidence grew until soon he was going off as well as anyone else—except perhaps Mad Dog—learning how to indy, nose bone and stalefish.

Manu was impressed. "You've got Mad Dog worried. You're a natural and he knows it," she said, one time when they were out together catching freshies. "Maybe you should ask Big Foot if you can come up the mountain with us this weekend. We're free riding all the way down and it's going to be something else."

She side-slipped away from him down the slope, swooping gracefully to kick back off a wind lip. Declan watched her carve the face, leaving a silvery trail in a single smooth line behind her. His gaze flicked back up to the three peaks towering over him.

"Guess I'm as ready as I'm ever going to be," he said aloud.

They assembled just before midday on the following Saturday at Moose Jaw. Manu, Mad Dog, and a big, thoughtful-looking kid with dreadlocks tied back, whom Declan assumed was Noah. The weather had improved enough for the sun to come out. The sunlight glinted on their snowboards as they stood about waiting, their breath smoking the air.

"Not you," Big Foot said to Declan. "You stay here and help Mary."

"But I thought, maybe," he paused, "I could go with you."

Manu nodded. "He's been putting in lots of practice."

But Big Foot's mind was made up.

"You are still not ready for such a journey, my young friend," Big Foot said. "One day perhaps, but not yet. The climb is too steep. The way down sheer. It would be too dangerous."

"He means no grommits!" Mad Dog jeered. "So why don't you shut up and leave it to the pros."

Declan stiffened. Something hot and scalding seemed to fill his head, burning the backs of his eyes and turning his face red. Not tears, anger. Seething fury. Frustrated, he could feel the others watching as he turned away.

Mad Dog's derisive whistles were cut short by Manu.

"What? Can't the drongo take a joke?" he heard Mad Dog say.

Declan kicked the front door closed behind him and ran up the stairs to his bedroom. But he wasn't beaten yet.

He watched them through the open attic window as Big Foot ran a check on their kit and the contents of their backpacks.

"Goggles?" "Check." "Gloves?" "Check." "Boots and spare socks?" "Check. Check."

"Crampons?" Big Foot held up the spiked, metal plates that they would strap to the soles of their feet for climbing on ice.

The clink of metal as they checked them off.

"Pack these things in your backpacks carefully," the old man said, "but leave your snowshoes until last."

He showed them where to strap the wide, lightweight plastic snowshoes—shaped like strange-looking tennis rackets—on the outside of their packs so they could be reached easily; he attached a spare pair to his own pack along with an extra coil of rope just in case.

"The first rule of the mountains—always be prepared," he said, speaking with authority. "You can lose a snowshoe or break a rope and find yourself in deep trouble.

"The weather, too, can change in the time it takes a bird to cross the sky." He fluttered his hand at the scribbles of cirrus cloud. "The speed of it can steal the breath from your body. A storm can rise like a ghost from the north. The temperature drop like a hunting hawk. Mist can creep from the trees, blinding your eyes so every step becomes difficult and dangerous."

Declan listened carefully. Especially when Big Foot explained their intended route, tracing the line of their ascent against the backdrop of Timberwolf's three jagged points: Razor Back, Thunder Ridge, and Timberwolf Top.

"To the Kutenai tribe they represented three spirits," the old man said and listed the Indian names in ascending order. "*Kukluknam*: Weariness. *Kukisak*: One Leg. *Kaklokalmiyit*: There-Is-No-Night-To-Him. Names of spirits that are difficult to say because they were meant to be sung not spoken. This was a sacred place and there are paintings hidden among the rocks on the mountain to prove it."

"Yeah, yeah," Mad Dog interrupted. "But when does the real action start?" He patted his board, then noticed Manu's angry look and quickly added, "Not that I'm going just for some mind-blowing free ride down. I'm just as stoked as anyone about the spirits of the mountain and all that stuff—more in fact. But you've got to admit, a hike like that and the run down is going to be pretty fat for the Pipe-Burner."

"Have you finished, my friend?" Big Foot asked.

Mad Dog decided he had and the old man thanked him with exaggerated politeness and picked up where he had left off.

They would take the cable-car to the Spotted

Walrus, he explained. Pick up the chairlift and take it to the Razor Back at 9,000 feet. It was only a short walk along the ridge and into the Back Bowls, then they would board down Snowdance Trail to Howling Wolf Rock, almost three thousand feet below.

"I'm going to nail that sucker one day," Mad Dog promised.

Noah looked startled. "You got a death wish or something?"

Mad Dog shrugged. "You've got to live it big while you're young."

Again, Big Foot waited until they quieted before going on. "From Howling Wolf Rock it is back to walking as we climb up through the woods on Thunder Ridge to the Refuge at 8,100 feet," he said. "You have all visited the Refuge in the summer when it is open as a base for climbers and walkers. In the winter it is cold, with few comforts. No electricity for light. No hot water for washing. Only an open fire to cook on and some blankets to keep you warm."

"What about a TV to expand our minds?" Mad Dog grinned.

"We will see who is laughing tomorrow, my confident friend," Big Foot said, beginning to sound annoyed.

"*Tomorrow*," Manu savored the word.

"Tomorrow," Big Foot echoed, "we cross the glacier and climb to the Timberwolf Top, which is more than 11,000 feet."

"Eleven thousand, four hundred and eighty-two feet to be exact," Noah corrected him with the air of someone who had studied the subject carefully. "At that altitude, the air is approximately thirty percent thinner. Every step we take is going to feel like five."

"Give it a rest, Dan Doom," Mad Dog hissed.

"Noah speaks the truth," Big Foot said. "Up there, the air will taste as dry as dust. It will suck the sweat from your skin and give you a thirst you cannot quench. So remember you must drink water regularly or suck snow for moisture."

"Or you'll dehydrate," Noah couldn't resist it.

Declan didn't hear all of Mad Dog's sarcastic reply because at that moment, Mary came bustling into his bedroom with her arms full of dirty laundry.

"I wondered where you had got to," she said. "You'll find some soup in the pot on the stove for your lunch. I'll be down in a little while to sort out some jobs for you to do this afternoon before the new guests arrive."

"Did Big Foot call Miss Everett about me?" he asked, casually.

"Miss Polly? I don't think so. Why?"

"No reason," Declan lied, looking back out the window.

Below, the others were shouldering their backpacks, their snowboards hooked into the straps across the back, bindings out. He watched as they formed into single file behind Big Foot, who leaned on an icepick as he led them away in the direction of the cable-car.

Mary muttered something about climbing a mountain of laundry and bustled out again. By the time her footsteps faded to the bottom of the attic stairs, Declan had already made up his mind to put his plan into action.

He changed quickly into his waterproof snow gear and laced his Mass-A-Taks over two pairs of socks. His gloves, goggles, and hat were in his pockets.

Halfway down the stairs, he caught a glimpse of Mary through an open door. She was tidying one of the guest rooms. Humming to herself as she moved about the room. He waited until she turned her back before moving down the stairs.

He left a note on the kitchen table, propped up. It didn't say where he was going, only that he would be back the next day and told her not to worry because he could look after himself. He stole three quick mouthfuls of soup directly from the pot simmering on the stove. Picked up his snowboard and quietly let himself out the back way without being noticed.

The man with the mirrored sunglasses by the cable-car shook his head.

"But I'm with Big Foot and the others," Declan pleaded, pointing at the cable-car fast disappearing over the first ridge of pine and spruce.

The man's mirrored eyes flashed. "No one goes up without a pass," he repeated. The words seemed to be branded on to his tongue alongside, "Eight to a car, please," and, "Have a nice day."

Rejected, Declan stepped back to let a crowd of skiers pass. Their hard boots rang on the metal steps as they climbed onto the platform where the cable-cars waited like big, brightly colored bubbles. "Eight to a car, please. Have a nice day," the operator said as they slotted their skis and boards into the racks on the side of the cable-car and stepped on board.

Declan edged closer, waiting for those sunglasses to stop mirroring his movements. Distracted, they turned away with a flash. It only took a moment for him to squeeze through the door before it slid shut, *scha-lunk*.

A jolt and suddenly they were moving.

The sun slanted through the window, warming the bubble and giving off a faint smell of plastic as Declan watched the cable-car station sink behind them. The man soon became a mirror-eyed ant and finally disappeared altogether as the ground dropped away below. The passengers sat patiently as the car swayed in the gentle breeze, rolling up its steeply slanting cable toward the trees and the ridge.

By the time the cable-car had reached the drop-off point near the Spotted Walrus, Big Foot and the others were already riding the chairlift up toward the Razor Back.

"You never heard of a line, kid?" the skier in front said as Declan tried to worm his way to the front of the line.

"But that's my mom," he lied, singling out the happy looking woman with blonde hair at the front.

"Is that so," the man said, unrelenting. "Well, I guess she must be my mom too."

"And mine," said another (who looked old enough to be her grandfather).

All those in earshot laughed.

Frustrated, Declan was forced to wait his turn. Watching the endless procession of tubular, metal chairs—each carrying two people—climbing at intervals up the hill. They returned, empty and bobbing on the steel cable. Swinging around the pylon with the whirling wheelhead to pick up two more from the platform by the wooden hut, before starting the long climb back up the hill.

The line seemed to move forward at an agonizingly slow pace and by the time he reached the front, Declan had lost sight of Big Foot and the others altogether.

His plan had been to shadow them all the way up to the Refuge, spend the night close by but undetected, then set off at dawn so he could be waiting for them at the top when they arrived. He couldn't wait to see the look on Big Foot's face. He was really going to enjoy asking Mad Dog what had kept him. But it was all going horribly wrong.

"Stop day-dreaming, kid!"

The warning came just as the double seat came swinging around behind him. He felt it bunt the backs of his legs and sat down heavily. The chair rocked alarmingly as it scooped him up and carried him away up the hill.

"Dumb kid'll probably fall out now," the man

said under his breath and pulled the safety bar down in front of them quickly.

Trapped, Declan watched the mountain slide under him. The trees gradually thinned out, becoming stunted and sparse, until they reached a line which, as if by some unspoken agreement with the rocks, they would not cross.

Here, the snow had heaped into deep overhangs, cornices that cushioned the crags. Perpendicular faces of bluish gray stone too sheer to be covered. Where wind and water had gnawed the rocks, and ice had thrust its cold, clear fingers deep into the crevices, prying them open until they cracked and tumbled.

Ahead, the Razor Back grew steadily. Its serrated edge slashing the sky, until the chairlift passed under the last of the T-shaped pylons and they reached the top. The safety bar came up, releasing him on to the mound of snow at the end of the chairlift. He slid to a stop by the cluster of warning signs that marked the high point.

The Razor Back was wider on top than it had looked. Easily big enough for the dozen or so skiers and snowboarders who stood around preparing for the long run down. But Big Foot and the others were not among them, so Declan shouldered his board and followed the dwindling trail of footprints to a sign that marked the start of Snowdance Trail with a black diamond. A few breathless steps more and a big, red sign screamed DANGER at him. A final warning informing him that he was entering the Back Bowls at his own risk. An area of high cliffs and the ever-present danger of avalanches.

Below, the town of Timberwolf was just a dark jumble beside the sparkling crystal of the frozen lake. A thickening mist was rising from the wooded slopes as he set off along the narrowing ridge watched only by the cyclops eye of the dying sun.

At first glance, Snowdance seemed impossibly steep. The trail sneaking down between chunks of granite poking out of the snow, before the angle became less extreme as it opened on to a wide slope thick with fresh powder.

Below, Declan could see four tracks slashed deep into the snow, crisscrossing each other in garland patterns. Neat and even. Like smooth sliding steps in some elaborate waltz. The sight of them gave him hope.

Gingerly, he edged his board down the steepest part until he reached the open slope, then carefully divided the trail into sections. Pausing after each short run to catch his breath, gulping greedily at the thin air. He picked the easiest lines, reading the slopes as if the contours were instructions worded in subtle shades of light and dark, until he reached the treeline once more.

It was darker among the trees down in the gullies where the shadows tinged the snow green. As the sun began to sink toward the mountains in the west, the temperature dropped with it and he saw the first traces of fog misting the warmer air trapped beneath the branches. It draped hazy tendrils like smoky feather boas from the pines and softened the crisp lines of the tree trunks.

He edged his board into the slope and licked at his cracked lips. They tasted sticky and sweet. He picked up a handful of snow. It was icy cold but it burned his parched tongue and he dropped it, stained pink with blood.

He moved on, but slid a little too far to his right and lost sight of the lifeline left by the others in the snow. Heart thumping, he panicked. Overcorrected. Drifted too far to his right and found himself in a thick patch of pine trees.

His tongue seem to be swelling by the second, making it even harder to breath. Dizzy, he edged his board so he could lean against a trunk. The warmth of his shoulder softened the amber trails that had frozen on its bark and his sleeve stuck like velcro as he pulled away. He was still making futile attempts to brush off the stickiness when the snow disappeared from beneath his board and he dropped into the tree hole.

It all happened so quickly. One moment he was standing there brushing, the next he was slithering down in a shower of loose snow. Wind roaring in his ears. Branches snapping and cracking like jumping jacks. A blur of bark. Pine needles stabbing his hands and face. Then a sudden jolt as his board became wedged.

The shock of it jumbled his thoughts to junk and it took a moment to gather them into some kind of order. Only then did he realize what had happened and how fortunate it had been that his board had stopped his fall.

What he had mistaken for the base of the tree was in fact halfway up the trunk. The rest of it, down to its roots, lay buried beneath the deep drifts. Where the snow had touched the trunk, however, it had melted away to form a narrow gap, bridged at the top by only a thin crust. Had he fallen much farther, he would have been unable to get out. Stuck, it would have only been a matter of time before he succumbed to the creeping cold and been buried alive.

Sobbing. Shaking. Sucking at the air in painful gasps. He managed to release his feet from the bindings and drag himself out. It took all his strength to pull up his board and he lay, exhausted, in the snow.

Only then did he notice how thick the mist had become, making the trees around him hazy and indistinct. And with the creeping mist came silence. Every sound was muffled, save that of his own ragged breathing. Numbing his senses, leaving him cold and feeling utterly alone.

Until gradually he became aware of someone calling his name.

"D e e e e e e e e e e c l a a a a a a a a a a a a n!"
"Deeeeeeeeeeeclaaaaaaaaaaaan!"

He lifted his head and listened. There it was again. Soft and soothing. Distant. Echoing as if it was coming from a far off place.

"Big Foot?" he called out—a raven's croak. Somehow, it didn't seem so important to be first to the top any more.

No reply.

He caught a glimpse of someone moving among the trees and heard the voice again.

"Deeeeeeeeeeeeeeeeeeclaaaaaaaaaaaaaaaaaan!"

The shadow vanished, only to reappear farther off.

"Wait! I'm over here!" The words came out short and puffed.

He struggled to his knees, then his feet, his boots sinking into the deep snow. He used his board to steady himself, leaning on it like a crutch. Tiny lights were popping before his eyes—silent mini-fireworks—and his heart felt as if it would thump its way right out of his chest.

He did not understand that he was hyperventilating. He did not know that the more he struggled for breath, the worse it would become. He was unaware that it was only a matter of time before he passed out.

Ahead of him, he could see other shadows. Pale and indistinct in the soupy light. Faces, he saw faces. Smiling faces. He gasped.

"Jaz? No it can't be! You're all—dead!"

The faces were swirling in a disordered whirl: B. J. and Jamal and Jaz and Tony. He stumbled toward them, leaning on his board as he stepped out of the trees onto a narrow ledge. A ledge that sloped down to disappear abruptly into the mist.

The shadows drifted away before him, misty wraiths shot through with colored light. He could hear the sound of laughter as they called to him:"Deeeeeeeeeeeeclaaaaaaaaaaaaan!" "Deeeeeeeeeeeeclaaaaaaaaaaaaan!"

"Jaz! Please come back!" he snatched at them with hooked fingers, but some primordial instinct forbade him from taking a step farther. So he could only stand and watch as his friends pirouetted away. Ephemeral. Siren voices fading. Until at last they were gone.

But even as he stood lost on the very edge of the unknown, he was not alone.

He could see eyes. Eyes in the gloom below the trees. Two points of pale green light, flecked yellow, with coal-black pupils shaped like almonds. Hunting eyes. Unblinking.

The giant wolf stood watching him, ears pricked, the rough of its gray mane dappled white.

Declan heard the deep rumble in the creature's throat, a rattle of air like a half-swallowed growl only louder, like distant thunder. His heart was squeezed by icy fingers as he waited for the snarling rush. The hideous howling run.

Seconds passed, stretching. Still the wolf did not move. It just stood watching him. Then without warning, it flattened its ears, turned, and trotted away into the mist.

The relief rocked Declan on his heels. He blinked at the creeping blackness that threatened to overwhelm him and tried to think clearly. He could still see the wolf. It had stopped farther up the slope and was looking back over its shoulder as if waiting for him to follow.

He took one shuffling step toward it. Paused, leaning heavily on his snowboard, and waited to see what it would do. Another step, then another, and soon the trees were crowding around him again. Spreading their branches over his head as they ushered him into the twilight zone. The wolf trotted on ahead again. Again it stopped and looked back, eyes shining brighter as the daylight faded.

"Why are you helping me?" he called.

The wolf growled threateningly at the sound of his voice. It turned and moved on quickly. Winding its way through the trees. Halting only when he fell too far behind. Letting him catch up before trotting on up the slope. Until suddenly Declan stumbled into a clearing.

Ahead the slope climbed steeply toward a ridge bare of trees. The wolf had vanished without trace. The snow was smooth and even, unblemished by a single paw print, and the thought of having lost the mysterious creature robbed him of what little strength he had left. His knees buckled and he sank into the soft, deep snow.

Declan wanted to sleep for ever and ever. His eyelids fluttered, touched, and settled as he began to drift.

He didn't know what brought him back, but he felt as if he had come from a faraway place where a warm wind blew. Suddenly his eyes were open again. He blinked at the half moon that had risen and perched on the shoulder of the mountain. Then he heard it—the cool, clear voice of the wolf. Howling. A haunting wail that seemed to echo for all eternity around the mountains. Calling him.

The wolf was standing at the top of the slope.

Its shaggy flank silvery gray in the moonlight. Its great head silhouetted against the half-eaten moon.

With one last, supreme effort, he dragged himself to his feet and, step by agonizing step, to the top of the snow ridge. By the time he had reached it, the wolf had gone. He crested the rise and saw two points of light in the distance. Squarer, perhaps. A little less green, a little more orange than yellow. And, strangest of all, at last, getting closer with every stumbling step he took.

They grew bigger and brighter, wider apart, until he realized they were no longer the eyes of the wolf, but windows. Small and square. Lit by the warm firelight inside. Set in the blank wall of a half-buried house that stuck out of the snow in the moonlight like the angled tail of a crashed spaceship.

He reached the door and pushed it open. He felt the warmth wash over him. Smelled the beans cooking. Saw the surprise on their faces. Big Foot, Manu, Mad Dog, and Noah. The rafters began to turn in a whirl. The floor rushed up. Then, nothing.

13

Declan woke with the dawn. The ashes were gray and cold in the fireplace. The only sound, the gentle breathing of the others as they slept, curled up on the camp beds, still fully clothed beneath the red survival blankets.

Only Big Foot was awake. Sitting cross-legged on the floor by the window, rocking gently back and forth, eyes closed as he faced the rising sun.

The blanket fell away as Declan stood up. The dizziness and headache had gone and his tongue had been softened by the sips of water and hot soup they had given him. Only his cracked lips and a few scratches and bruises told the tale of his ordeal and of how lucky he had been.

He stood and watched the dawn peel back the edges of the sky. The morning light shimmering on the angled slopes.

"I saw the wolf," he said to Big Foot, quietly so the others wouldn't hear.

Big Foot stopped rocking back and forth. Sat still for a moment, then started again.

The others stirred beneath the blankets. Only Mad Dog slept on, his brand-new boots sticking out from the end of the camp bed. Manu got up, hair tousled and blanket wrapped around her shoulders as she helped Noah stoke life into the fire.

"I said, I saw the wolf," Declan tried a little louder. "It saved my life."

They were all listening now, even Mad Dog.

"You should not have followed us, my young friend," Big Foot said, without opening his eyes. "It was dangerous. It was wrong."

"I know. I'm sorry," Declan said. "But I had to, don't you see. I wanted to prove that I'm just as good as the others."

Big Foot nodded, but said nothing.

So Declan told them what had happened, from the moment he had left Moose Jaw to the moment he saw the shadows in the mist and the wolf watching him.

"Sounds like mountain-sickness to me," Noah pronounced his verdict. "Dehydration causes headaches. Breathlessness causes hyperventilation. The body's carbon dioxide level drops, the alkaline level in the blood rises. It's obvious. *Everyone* knows the kidneys slowly excrete the excess alkaline, resulting in the lowering of the blood's pH level."

"Will you shut up about all that stuff!" Mad Dog said.

"All I'm saying," Noah said, "is that mountain-sickness makes you breathless and dizzy. So I'm not surprised Declan started seeing things—hallucinating."

"Why won't you believe me?" Declan said. "I heard voices calling to me and the next thing I knew I was standing on this narrow ledge with the trees behind me."

"Sounds like Howling Wolf Rock," Manu said.

"And that's where I saw the wolf," Declan continued. "It was awesome. As tall as me, bigger maybe, and its eyes shone like lights in the dark. It trotted off through the trees, then waited for me to follow. I even heard it howl."

Big Foot's eyes snapped open.

They shifted uneasily and glanced at one another.

"Like I said," Noah spoke in barely more than a whisper, "mountain-sickness *can* cause hallucinations."

"Nice one, drongo," Mad Dog said to Declan as he settled his goggles over his eyes. "First you follow us and nearly get yourself wiped like the true grommit you are. Then you spook everyone out with a load of bull about voices and shadows in the mist. And now you've gone and said you heard the wolf howling. Have you any idea what that means around here?"

Declan remembered something Manu had said in the shop. "You mean about it howling before something bad happens on the mountain?"

"At last you've got something right, drongo," Mad Dog said. "Big Foot is into all that Indian stuff. He sees it as a bad omen. That's why he's called off the climb. Thanks to you, I don't get to go up there where the cornices are fat, packed, and ready for the drop." He pointed toward the peak then poked Declan's shoulder with the same finger. "I don't like it when some city kid comes in and starts messing up my life!"

Mad Dog glared and let his board take him down the hill, gradually picking up speed as he headed for a patch of snow-covered rocks. Declan watched as he kicked off the top in a powder burst, dipping the nose of his board, and leaning back, nose boning out of sight as he dropped down the hill toward the glacier.

"It wasn't bull!" Declan called after him, even though he knew Mad Dog couldn't hear.

Big Foot had delayed his decision until after breakfast. He had considered the situation carefully, then decided not to continue with the main climb. This, he had said, was because of the dangers of taking Declan any higher so soon after having suffered mountain-sickness, but they had all noticed the change that had come over him since Declan had mentioned the wolf.

"We will cross the glacier to Timberwolf Top and descend that way," the old man said, looking troubled. "The slopes will be easier than those of Thunder Ridge, which are heavy with snow. The danger of avalanches is too great, my friends."

It seemed the only other way to reach the foot of the mountain from where they were was on foot via Howling Wolf Rock. Not surprisingly, no one seemed too keen to go that way after what Declan had said.

The sense of foreboding hung in the air like a cloying smell as they packed up their things. They left the Refuge ready for the next people and set off down to the glacier.

The slope was wide and open. The snow deep on the ridges, forming a series of moguls and kick-backs which, one by one, they took. Declan followed Manu as she went gliding down the hill, like a snow-sprite sliding on magic trails, until they carved to a halt by the side of the glacier.

The glacier stretched away before them to the other side of the valley. Wide, but not as flat as it had appeared from a distance. A huge highway of ice strewn with snow-covered rocks, some as big as cars, rising out of its mountain cirque just below Timberwolf Top. Squeezing down the mountain. A giant floe of ice moving imperceptibly, but with all the awesome, unstoppable force of nature behind it.

Time and the enormous weight of the ice had ground out the rocks beneath the glacial sole to form a natural halfpipe in the rock rising to sharp ridges down either side. The ice plucking the rocks from their mountain beds with ease. Flowing. Stretching until the surface cracked into crevasses or dropped over a rock step in the beautiful chaos of an icefall. Until eventually, without appearing to have moved at all, it reached the frozen lake at its nose: its journey's end.

"Big Foot told me to give you these," Mad Dog said, dropping the spare snowshoes at Declan's feet in disgust. "We wouldn't want you falling behind and getting lost again, now would we? You'd probably see a bunch of flying pigs." He laughed at his own joke and stomped off.

"Don't worry about Mad Dog," Manu said,

when he had gone. "I think he's jealous of you."

"Jealous? Of *me*? Don't be stupid. What's he got to be jealous about?"

"Plenty."

"You really think so?"

She nodded, but her smile faded to awkwardness as if another thought had struck her. "Then again, maybe it's something else."

Declan was disappointed. He had enjoyed the compliment. "How do you mean *something else*?"

"Something to do with what you saw him doing in the shop."

"Oh, that," Declan said, embarrassed. "Guess I made a fool of myself, huh?"

"Maybe," she mused, "maybe not."

Declan was too busy strapping on his snowshoes—and wondering if Big Foot had known all along who would be using them—to notice Manu's gaze settle on Mad Dog's new boots.

Declan shouldered his board and waited as the others hooked theirs into the straps of their backpacks and formed up in single file. Big Foot had decided to cross the glacier a little way up from an icefall, where the ice spilled over a step in the rock and broke into giant blocks, heaped up like discarded bricks.

Declan found the strange, tennis racket shoes unwieldy at first, flapping around on the soles of his boots, but he soon discovered they made walking much easier. They spread his weight on the snow and stopped his feet from sinking in. Walking became less tiring. His breathing easier and less ragged. As he walked, his spirits began to lift, despite the gloomy mood that prevailed among the rest of the party.

Somehow, just by being up there, he felt as if he had conquered something. Not so much the mountain, the weight of which he still felt, but more something inside himself. His fear of the unknown, perhaps. He wasn't too sure. But whatever it was, he found he could look at the world around him in a different way.

Suddenly, the peaks reminded him of awesome waves. They stood frozen against the sky. Their foaming white crests splashing glacial drops as they rolled endlessly toward some half-imagined shore. *This* world seemed new. Different from the old one he had known. A brighter, cleaner place where his past could be forgotten and he could be happy again. And yet, even this new world was filled with hidden danger.

"Crevasse!" the warning shivered back down the line and they came to a sudden halt.

A snaking crack in the ice barred their way. Big Foot tested the snow with his icepick, looking for a way around. A mysterious light radiated out of it, a deep blue glow of refracted sunlight, and Declan couldn't resist a closer look. He peered over the edge. The patterns on the ice seemed to ripple and he could see icicles stretching into the deep, hanging down like magnificent inverted cathedrals made entirely out of crystal.

"I knew a slider who fell down one of them once," Mad Dog said, grinning. "By the time the rescue guys reached him, the hole in the ice had started to close up. They say it squeezed and squeezed him until his eyes popped out." He laughed. "He was a drongo too."

"Why don't you leave him alone?" Manu said.

Mad Dog sneered at Declan. "It's becoming a habit—you always hiding behind her."

Declan was about to deny it angrily, when Big Foot announced they would have to go back the way they had come.

"There are many hidden cracks," the old man said, when he found no obvious way around the hole. "We must try farther up."

So they retraced their steps—Declan and Mad Dog glaring at each other—and climbed higher up the glacier, looking for a safer route. This time with more success. They made good progress and could soon pick out details on the slope on the other side. Configurations in the rocks that stepped up toward a series of smooth snow-covered slopes, below the peak.

"Will you look at them," Mad Dog said. His eyes glittered as he followed hidden lines down the slope like an artist contemplating a blank canvas. "Awesome, man. Truly *awesome*."

Declan looked up at the slopes rising before him. The wind had shaped and smoothed them. They were clean and untouched. Empty. And suddenly the voice in his head was whispering again, reminding him of another, darker place.

"Clean skins," the voice whispered breathlessly.

108

Soon after they reached the other side, Big Foot called a halt so they could rest. They sat, perched on some rocks poking up out of the snow at the foot of a long slope, eating chocolate cookies and swigging water from plastic flasks as they listened to Big Foot explaining their route down.

Declan felt someone tap him on the shoulder and turned to find Mad Dog.

"You coming, drongo?" Mad Dog whispered.

"Where?"

"Keep your voice down!" Mad Dog indicated up the slope with a nod of his head. "You want to leave your mark on some fresh stuff, don't you? Go where no slider has ever been?"

They were words Declan had heard before and they sent a shiver through him. Suddenly he was back on that sheer face above the tracks. His head filled with darkness. He heard the wheels of the train on the track. The flames leapt up.

"No!" the word burst from his lips.

They all looked at him in surprise.

He smiled weakly. "Sorry."

The others turned back to the map Big Foot was drawing with his icepick in the snow.

"Forget you, man," Mad Dog hissed in Declan's ear.

"Forget you too!"

"You're just yellow."

"Maybe I am and maybe I'm not," Declan said. "But at least I'm not dumb enough to trust *you*." He turned his back on Mad Dog and it felt good.

Declan ignored Mad Dog's mutterings and listened to Big Foot instead. The old man was pointing out their route down on the snow map with the handle of his icepick. Down through some arrow-shaped trees. Pointing out trails with names like Songline and Brown Bear. Past Macreedy's Point and Native Cat and Muster Ridge. Until eventually he used his pick to cut a straight line in the snow. This, he said, was the road. "Where Mary will be waiting with the Land Cruiser to pick us up."

They buzzed with excitement as they exchanged their snowshoes for boards and lined up for the long run down. Only then did they notice that Mad Dog was missing.

"I knew he'd do something stupid," Manu said.

Big Foot found the trail of footprints leading away from the rocks and up the slope. The tracks quickly disappeared over the shoulder, then reappeared higher up. He shaded his eyes and scanned the slopes above.

"I fear I was wrong about the one you call Mad Dog, my young friends," the old man said grimly. "He was not ready for this and now I fear the Great Wolf has chosen him to test us all."

"There!" Declan saw him first.

Mad Dog had climbed to a spot about a hundred and fifty feet above a rocky cliff topped by a heavy cushion of snow. He had strapped on his board and they could see him taking a long look at the slope below the cliff where he would be landing.

"If he makes that jump, he'll bring down the cornice, for sure," Noah said. "The whole slope could go."

"He's just crazy enough to get us all swallowed by the Wolf," Manu said.

Declan studied the slopes around them. Above, they were steep—at angles of 40 degrees or more—dropping into the natural depression where they were standing. An open-ended bowl shape, which would funnel any avalanche breaking out above straight down on them.

Big Foot had seen the danger too. "Follow me! We must fly like birds on the wind!" he said, leading the way.

They obeyed without hesitation. Moving fast. Sliding down the slope to gain momentum, then cutting back sharply toward the shoulder that formed one side of the natural bowl. Declan was the last to reach the safety of the ridge. He slid to a stop by Manu just as Mad Dog went over the top.

Mad Dog took off with a *Whoop!* that ricocheted around the peaks, until it sounded like he was just one of a crazy pack. He went huge off the top of that rock. It was awesome. He went rocketing through the air, trailing powder snow behind in a smoky white blur as if he had outrun his own soul. He corkscrewed through 360 slow-motion degrees, found perfect balance, then dropped in for a landing that sent rivers of snow shimmering down the slope all around him.

"Unreal!" Noah said.

And for one, fleeting moment, they thought the slope had held. Then they saw the crack.

It appeared a few feet below Mad Dog's board. Thin, growing fat. Mad Dog saw it and carved away in a tight turn that took him clear of danger. But he had already set a chain of events in motion which no force on earth could stop.

Unseen, the crack spread down from the surface, through the harder layers of snow packed below, until it reached a softer layer of sugar snow and spread out in deadly veins. The whole slab became unstable. It cracked. Lurched. Held for a second longer, then dropped.

What had been smooth and even was suddenly transformed into a churning mass. Large blocks of hard-packed snow cracked into smaller pieces and these into smaller pieces still. After a few yards, the chunks were traveling at more than thirty miles an hour and accelerating, puffing up clouds of powder that engulfed everything as they thundered down the slope, carrying all before them.

The avalanche swallowed the rocks where they had just been sitting, picked up speed and swept on past them down the slope. By the time it slammed into the trees, it had reached speeds of one hundred and thirty miles an hour. A raging torrent. Snapping whole stands of pines, many of which had stood for two hundred years, carrying them away like twigs.

The sight of it left Declan feeling breathless, yet strangely elated. Dizzy in a light-headed sort of way, which only the passing of terrible and immediate danger can induce.

A tremor ran through him.

It was only the faintest of vibrations, running up through his board into the soles of his feet, but it was enough. He had felt a similar tremor before, as the train had slithered out of that dark hole of a tunnel down on the tracks.

"There's another one coming!" he gasped.

Manu cocked her head and listened. Her face went pale. The second avalanche had been triggered by the vibrations of the first. It had broken out just below Timberwolf Top. Much bigger than the first, it gathered momentum. Sliding down the upper slopes, hidden from view by the slopes above them.

No time.

They banked away down the slope in close formation. Dropping fast. Swooping, a doomed flight in controlled freefall, jinking down the wooded slopes, with the trees quickstepping back up the hill in ranks like ground troops off to face the enemy.

Behind them, the wave of snow burst over the rocky outcrop, exploding into the air as if it wanted to prove it could jump higher than Mad Dog, then poured on down the slope. Thundering onto the rocks. Flooding the natural bowl and spilling over the ridge where they had just been standing. From there it spread wide and flat to drown them in an endless sea of liquid white.

Declan heard a startled cry and saw Manu go down as her board snagged on the root of a tree. She went spinning away helplessly. Slithering into a drift by some trees that clung to the top of an outcrop of rock. Instinctively, he dug the toe edge in deep, bringing the nose of his board around. The Thunderbird shuddered beneath his feet, carving into a turn as he went after her.

By the time he reached her and had slid to a stop, Manu was already on her feet. "Keep going!" she shouted above the noise.

"Not without you!"

She just shook her head and pointed past him.

Nothing could have prepared Declan for the sight that met his eyes when he looked back.

The whole mountain above them seemed to move. Seething. Shimmering. The avalanche's awesome beauty disguising the white death it brought. He thought some great hunting animal had suddenly leapt out of hiding and was bounding down the slope toward them. Racing the wind. Stretching its giant claws ahead, ready to rip and tear at anything in its path. And in its roar he heard the voice of the wolf once more.

"Jump!" Declan shouted, dragging Manu to the edge. "It's our only hope!"

They went together, dropping fast to land in the deep snow at the base of the outcrop. They just had time to drag themselves, boards still attached to their feet, into the hollow of the overhang before the avalanche hit.

The weight of thousands of tons of snow on the move made the very bones of the earth quake. The mountain trembled at its awesome power as it burst over the top of them. Cascading in a frozen torrent. Eating up the world and drinking the blue of the sky.

Declan plugged his ears with his fingers and screamed into its deafening noise. It obliterated his senses, robbing him of his sight and sense of smell, and numbing him until he could feel nothing but the endless bone-jarring thump of the blocks of ice and splintered trees as they thudded into the ground just beyond the mouth of the hollow where they cowered.

As the great mass rolled on, wreaking its havoc down the mountainside below, the beast inside it seemed to sense that somehow they had escaped. It roared its fury in a blast of frozen breath. A swirling back draft of air slapped them down into the snow like a mighty, invisible claw, knocking the breath from their lungs and plucking at their very souls.

Suddenly—incredibly—the beast had gone.

Silence. Ears ringing, they sat and blinked at the carnage around them.

"So that's what it's like being swallowed by the Wolf," Declan said.

14

"I should have stopped him."

"Impossible. That's why he's called Mad Dog."

"But I knew what he was going to do," Declan said. "It was obvious—the clean skins."

Manu looked puzzled. "What are clean skins?"

"They're . . ." Declan thought for a moment, then shrugged. "Forget it. It's a long story."

They were all safely back in Timberwolf, with only Noah the worse for their experience.

"I busted my leg," he had said, when they found him near Macreedy's Point.

But he had been lucky. Big Foot too. The main slip of snow had followed the contours of the slope and passed over the outcrop of rock under which Declan and Manu had been hiding. Big Foot and Noah had reached the safety of a knoll and the smaller slip, which had pursued them, passed right by.

It was only later, when they had all met up again and had been looking for Mad Dog that Noah had slipped and fallen into the hole.

Noah said it didn't hurt, but he had grimaced as they pulled him out. So they splinted his leg with Big Foot's icepick, then rigged up a small sled by tying two of the backpacks to the bindings of Noah's snowboard to form a seat. Big Foot fixed a rope to the makeshift sled and used it to lower Noah down the steep slopes.

Halfway down, Mad Dog had appeared on the horizon. He was traveling fast and seemed totally oblivious of the trouble he had caused. They saw him going off a ridge, dropping like a sky diver, then disappearing into the trees below. It seemed nothing was going to stop him from having a good time.

They had caught up with him, eventually. He was sitting in the back of the Land Cruiser with his boots resting on the seat in front of him, telling Mary how wonderful he was. He denied all knowledge of the avalanche or how the snow slide had been started.

"You can't blame me for every stupid thing that happens on the mountain," he growled.

"And what about Noah?" Manu asked.

"How was I supposed to know the nerd had busted his leg?"

Manu gave up in frustration. Mad Dog just sat grinning until Big Foot made him give up his place so Noah could lie along the backseat of the truck. By the time they had loaded their gear into the back, they found there wasn't enough room for them all. One would have to walk, and everyone knew who deserved to most.

"But it's three miles back to town!" Mad Dog whined.

"Then the walk will be good to clear your head," Big Foot said. "Maybe you will come to see that only the greatest fools think they know everything."

And with that they drove away.

It did not take long for Manu to work out how they were going to get their revenge on Mad Dog. It was time, she said, to show Carl Martin that he was not quite as hot as he thought he was.

"And you're going to help us do it," she said to Declan as they stood in the shop.

"Me? How?"

"By beating him in the Pipe-Burner Competition next week," she said.

"The Pipe! No way!"

"You've got to," Manu insisted. "It's all arranged. We had a bit of trouble getting you in at the last minute, but Papa pulled a few strings and the organizers agreed to let you take Noah's place."

"But we're talking major league!" he said. "FIS qualifier!"

"That's why you're going to have to train so hard," Manu said. "We've only got one week, but I know you can do it." She turned to her father who was standing behind the counter. "And you have something to help him win, haven't you Papa?"

Monsieur Jonquiere nodded and came round the counter. He took a new freestyle board down from the rack and cradled it lovingly in his arms. It was a brand-new Thunderbird Mark V.

"I would like you to 'ave this," he said. "So when you are famous, I will be able to say you started out on one of my boards!" He became serious. "But most of all, it is just a small token of my gratitude for saving my little Manu's life. For that I will always be grateful."

Declan felt totem-pole-tall.

The week passed very quickly. For Declan, it was a seemingly endless blur. Each morning he had to be up before everyone else so he could be sure all the work at Moose Jaw was done before he went out to the slopes. Manu helped where she could, but she had school most days so Declan worked alone a lot. But he was pleased with the jumps he was making and decided that, if everything went right on the day, he had a chance. And that made him feel good too.

As the day for the competition approached, Timberwolf began to fill up with people. Competitors and spectators alike, all coming for the weekend's events. Moose Jaw was full, apart from two rooms that Big Foot insisted should be set aside for some very special visitors. Who, he would not say. Only that it would be a surprise.

An even bigger surprise came that evening, however, when, without even being asked, Big Foot decided Declan should go to the concert being held beside the frozen lake.

All week the rumor had been going around that the band Purple Crayon was in Timberwolf. They were supposed to be at the concert that evening. Top Nigel had been billed as lead, along with a couple of local bands.

Secretly, Declan had been longing to go. To be allowed to seemed too good to be true and left him wondering if, sooner or later, he would wake up and find his new, exciting life was all just a dream.

"I once told you that the day would come when you would be ready to tell others why you came to Timberwolf, my young friend," Big Foot said, when the moment came for Declan to go to the concert. "I want you to remember this when you see Manu and Noah tonight."

"Tell Manu? No way!" Declan said, shaking his head. "If I did that she would hate me."

"Sometimes the ghosts of the past can come back to haunt us," the old man said. "They cling to our thoughts with their bony fingers and try to pull us down into the shadows where only they belong. Sometimes the only way to break free is by facing them, as you did the mountain."

"But how?"

"By trusting others to help you. Others like Manu and Noah." Big Foot laid a hand on his shoulder. "Friendships built on secrets and lies are like houses built on sand—they do not last."

And with that Big Foot walked away. Declan watched him go, then turned slowly and stepped out into the cold night air. The old man's words were to stick with him all evening.

A large crowd had gathered in front of a stage that had been erected on the edge of the frozen lake. Under the white glare of the lights, he found Manu chatting with some friends. Noah was there, too, leaning on his crutches, his plaster-cast leg attracting the attention of anyone with a pen and a rude message. He seemed oblivious of the damage they were doing. He was too busy explaining the laws of physics behind the forces that cause avalanches. It didn't seem to bother him that no one was listening.

The lights dimmed and someone pointed up at the slopes above the town. A procession of skiers carrying torches was coming down the mountain. The lights trickled through the velvet darkness in a fiery snake, winking as they passed under the branches of trees, before finally disappearing as the skiers reached the edge of town.

Suddenly: lights, music, dry ice, action and the first of the bands hit the stage.

Declan was swept up by the crowd and carried irresistibly toward the stage. But as he stood there with all those people dancing around him, he realized the invisible barrier was still in place. It separated him from them, just as surely as it had that day at the Spotted Walrus, and suddenly he knew it always would unless he did something about it. Only then did he understand what Big Foot had been trying to tell him. Only then did he know what he had to do to be free.

"Manu, I have to talk to you!" he shouted above the throbbing beat.

"Can't it wait?" She was dancing.

"It's important."

He led the way out through the crowd and up the slope to the corner of the main street.

"Top Nigel will be on soon," she complained, "and I want to be near the front for the Purples."

Declan felt as if something cold and heavy had somehow managed to curl itself up in the pit of his stomach. He turned away from her, looking out over the crowd to the frozen lake beyond. The spotlights had turned the ice to diamonds.

"What would you say if someone had done something bad?" he said after a long pause.

"That depends."

"On what?"

"On what it was."

Declan swallowed the tennis ball that seemed to be bobbing up and down in his throat. "Well, what if it was something really bad, but it had just sort of got out of control."

"You mean like a stupid joke?"

Declan sighed, "Sort of."

She looked at him suspiciously. "You haven't done something to make Big Foot mad, have you?"

"No, look this is serious," he said. "That's why I've got to tell you."

Declan paused to let a group of people pass by, heading for the concert, and was about pick up where he had left off when Mad Dog came loping around the corner.

"Well, well, looky here," Mad Dog said, slurring his words. Declan could smell the beer on his breath. "If it isn't the drongo who thinks he can beat me tomorrow." He laughed, gave Declan a shove that sent him staggering back, and turned his attention to Manu.

"So you've told your papa all about me, have you, girl? Told him the avalanche was all my fault, when it was only an accident. Well, see if I care! Because tomorrow I'm going to win the

Pipe and then I won't need you or him or his stupid job. And then I won't even bother with any of you."

"Leave her alone!" Declan said.

"In your face, man!"

It was then that Declan's world fell apart.

Out of the corner of his eye, he caught a glimpse of someone getting out of a car across the street. He recognized the pale, drawn face immediately.

"Redback," he breathed the reporter's name as if it meant death.

Mad Dog frowned and followed the line of Declan's gaze. "Who's Redback?"

Declan dragged his eyes away from the reporter and shook his head. "No one. I mean, I've never seen him before in my life."

Mad Dog's grin turned into a leer. "It don't look that way to me, drongo," he said, grabbing Declan's jacket. "Maybe we should go and have a word with the dude. Find out what's going on."

Hooked, Declan panicked as he had done in Fat Arnold's. He dropped low, twisted sharply, and broke free from Mad Dog's grip.

"I've got to go," he said, backing away. "I've just remembered something—something important."

"But what about the concert?" Manu did not sound happy.

"No! Sorry. I've got to go."

He turned on his heel and tried not to run as he made his way up the street, keeping his face hidden in case Redback spotted him.

"Always knew there was something weird

about you, drongo," Declan heard Mad Dog call
after him.

Declan picked up the cans of spray paint and
cleared the nozzles with quick squirts. He took a
deep breath, stepped up to the wall of his attic
bedroom and began to spray.

He slashed the three peaks of Timberwolf
Mountain in a ragged line up the sloping wall to
the apex of the ceiling. He edged the white peaks
in black and stood on his bed to add the ultra vi-
olent swirl of a giant orange sun. Drawing from a
map in his mind, he marked off the places he
knew so well. And over them he sprayed the head
of a giant wolf, snarling silver trails of saliva from
its jagged teeth.

The door flew open and he saw Big Foot standing framed against the light. Silent. Shadowy.
Arms folded. Angry. Mary, Manu, and the others
crowded in behind. A man with a pale, drawn
face pushed past them into the room and pointed
an accusing finger:

"Everyone is going to know what kind of filth
you really are!" he said. "Filth! Filth! Filth—
filth—filth—filth—filth—filth!"

Declan woke up sweating, his blankets screwed
into a ball. He sat up in bed and looked around.
The walls of his room were clean, but his relief
was only temporary.

It was still early, but he dressed quickly, slipping on his snowboarding gear for the competition. He remembered his special competitor's pass, picked up his new board, and bumped into Big Foot halfway down the stairs.

"Last night—there was a man," Declan explained breathlessly. "A journalist. I think he's looking for me."

"He was here," Big Foot said, "asking questions, but I sent him away."

"I can't let him find me or he'll spoil everything. That's why I've got to hide. He'll never find me on the mountain."

A pause. Big Foot smiled a sad smile, then shook his head.

"No one can hide forever," he said, steadying Declan with a big bony hand. "Do you remember the way you faced the mountain, my young friend? Do you remember the courage it gave you?" He waited for Declan to nod before continuing. "Well, the time has come to test that courage. If you believe in yourself, you will overcome any enemy and the truth will shine out of you like the sun."

"Do you really think so?"

Big Foot nodded. "But you must speak to Manu before this journalist does. It is better that she learns the truth from your own lips. You have enough time before Miss Polly arrives. She is bringing your mother and father to watch you in the competition."

"Mom? Dad? Coming to watch *me*?"

Big Foot nodded and dug deep into his pocket. "And I have five dollars that says you can win if you give it your best shot."

"But that's my money!"

Big Foot chuckled. "All the more reason for you to win."

Declan's confidence lasted all the way to The Snow Shack. He hammered on the locked door and brought Monsieur Jonquiere hurrying. But Manu's father did not smile when he saw him nor was he willing to open the door.

"It's me, Mr. Jonquiere—Declan!" he called through the glass.

The door opened a little way. "What do you want?"

Declan was surprised. "I've come to see Manu."

"Well, she's not 'ere. She went out, early. And I don't blame 'er," he said. "Carl brought a visitor late last night. A journalist—from the newspapers. He told us all about you. It seems you are a thief and a liar after all. And when I remembered 'ow I found you in my shop it all started to make sense."

"Sense? No! You've got it all wrong."

The disappointment was written all over Monsieur Jonquiere's face. "I said I would always be grateful to you for saving my Manu's life, so I repay that debt by letting you go now without calling the police. But if you call yourself Manu's friend you will leave 'er alone. It would be better if you never saw 'er again."

And then the man who had been congratulating him only a few days before shut the door in his face.

Blood pumping, heart beating, hard breathing,

slow motion run, run, run, running. Declan's boots thumped into the ground as he ran back to Moose Jaw. His head was full of molten thoughts. Raging.

Miss Everett's bright red Ford was parked by the Land Cruiser. He saw his dad. His mother. Miss Everett chatting to Big Foot and Mary.

"You lied! All of you!" He was shouting. "There's no such thing as a second chance. Not for *me*. There never was. There never will be!"

They were saying things. Coming toward him. He backed away.

"Why can't everyone leave me alone!"

Declan turned and ran. He reached the cable-car and used his competitor's card to push his way to the front.

"Eight to a car, please," the man with the mirrored eyes said. "Have a nice day."

The door closed. *Scha-lunk*. Imprisoned. His life hung suspended as that cable-car crawled slowly to the top. The door opened and he burst out into the watery sunlight again.

The competitors were already gathering at the Spotted Walrus. Chatting. Laughing. Unaware of the seething turmoil inside the head of the kid who pushed through them.

"Have you seen Manu?" Declan kept asking. Only to be answered with blank stares and shrugs.

Below, beyond the pine trees, Declan could see spectators lining the halfpipe. It had been cordoned off and festooned with brightly colored advertisements strung along the rope fences.

"There he is, Mr. Redback!" It was Mad Dog's voice. "I said you would find him here. Now what about that sponsorship you promised?"

"We'll talk about that later," Redback growled.

A camera flashed in Declan's face. He blinked the brightness of it from his eyes and found himself looking into that pale face again.

Redback smiled, slow and easy. "Thanks for that, kid," he said. "I needed a good photo of you enjoying yourself. My readers are going to love this. The social services sending filth like you on vacation instead of locking you up where you belong."

Everyone was looking now. Staring. Accusing eyes were all around. Redback's camera flashed again. Mad Dog was grinning. But worst of all was the sight of Manu's face in the crowd. She was frowning and the confusion showed clearly in her dark eyes.

"I tried to tell you," Declan blurted. "Last night. I wanted to tell you. You *have* to believe me."

"I don't know what to believe any more," she said.

Declan stared and suddenly he felt strangely distant from her. It was as if that invisible barrier had sprung up between them and it was growing higher with every second that passed. It seemed Big Foot had lied about her, too.

Declan rubbed furiously at the tears that had begun to trace scalding lines down his face. The shame of showing his weakness was too much for him to bear. He pushed his way through the crowd and closed his ears to Redback's taunts.

Only Mad Dog blocked his path. "Boy does Manu hate you, drongo," he said and laughed in his face. "Guess you should have known you never could beat me. Not in the Pipe, not in anything. Because you're nothing, man. Nothing."

And suddenly Declan knew Mad Dog was right.

Declan cut his board into the fresh powder, digging in on the edge where the wind had sculpted faces in the ice. The pale, lifeless faces of his friends. Jaz, Jamal, Tony and B. J.

"You knew I would come back *here*, didn't you?" he said calmly. "You always did."

Silence. Only the wind.

Alone, he stood on Howling Wolf Rock. Snowdance had brought him down from the Razor Back, down through the trees to that narrow, snow-covered ledge where he had stood once before. Then the awesome drop had been shrouded in mist. Now he could see what it would be like to run with the Wolf.

"OK, you win," he said. "So let's do it!"

"Do it! Do it! Do it!" the siren voices called.

And even though he knew it was only his own voice echoing back to him, he shivered. It was as if the UXTs had reached from beyond the grave and fastened their icy, lifeless fingers around him, pulling him to the edge.

High up on the slope behind, he could see sliders cutting down from the Razor Back. Slashing deep lines in the snow. Zigzagging as they worked down the sheer white face of Snowdance. It was Big Foot and the others coming for him.

Too late.

All around him, the mountains shimmered in the sunlight. Piled up like awesome waves rolling toward that distant shore. The bright clean place he had longed to find.

This was his dream, shattered.

"Life sucks," he said, and the words tasted bitter in his mouth. "You taught me that, Jaz." He took a deep breath. "So I guess I'll see you guys later."

"Later! Later! Later!" they shrieked.

He shifted his weight and side-slipped down the slope to the edge. He was ready to run with the Wolf. He was ready to race the dead.

The colors swirled before his eyes. Bright and vibrant. Shining white against spinning blue. He was flying. An eagle on the wing. A Thunderbird spitting lightning fire.

The slope rushed up to meet him, smacking into the underside of his board. The ferocity of the jolt knocked the breath out of him. He kissed the wind lip. The abyss opened up before him. Desperately, he cut the heel edge of his board into the snow, slashing back from the edge in a sick 90-degree turn, and dropped neatly into the jaws of the Wolf. Too fast.

The rocks jumped up all around him, leaping higher, snapping at his heels and biting chunks out of the edge of his board. He fought to keep his balance. But the angle was too extreme. The slope too sheer. Gradually, inexorably, he began to lose it.

The Thunderbird disintegrated beneath his feet. Robbed of its wings, it died in flight. Declan stayed on his feet a moment longer before he fell. His back slammed in hard, robbing him of what little breath he had left as the slope whisked him away. The snow shoot turned into a giant ride. The Slide of Death.

A small tree loomed up in front of him. He made a grab for it, but his gloves slipped off. He watched helplessly as it whipped away and accelerated up the slope, dwindling to a tiny speck before disappearing altogether. He felt the rocks as they thumped into him. They bounced him from side to side, tossing him around like a rag doll. And all he could think was that he was going to die and it didn't seem to be hurting.

He was floating now. Untouchable. Lazily drifting on a warm, scented breeze. Nothing seemed important any more.

He could see the white tops of the mountains against the sky and thought he caught a glimpse of Jaz and the others, laughing and joking as they sprayed up the clouds.

Then, before him, a great gray wolf appeared at the bottom of the slope. Its noble head raised. Its eyes shining out of the face of a huge rock, watching over him. He reached out and touched its mane and the world stopped with an awesome thud.

When Declan opened his eyes, he was lying at the bottom of a tall cliff of gray stone. A monument. It vaulted away above him to end abruptly, capped in pure white snow. There, on that rock face that had, since time immemorial, looked out over the valley, he saw the rock paintings.

The great gray wolf stood surrounded by men and animals. Figures etched in black and white and yellow ocher, fading into the rock. Giant snorting bulls. Elk and deer. Bears and beaver. And people dancing. Man and nature together. Whirling across some vast, ancient land where eagles turned on the wing beneath the sun, moon, and the stars. And over them stood the three peaks of the great mountain.

Declan looked up at that bright, clean world and smiled. He was still smiling as he closed his eyes.

The three totem poles stood sharp-edged against the early morning sun. Charlie, Big Bird, and Sad Face stood as tall as trees. The pale light captured in droplets of dew that had gathered in the corners of their eyes and along their beaks and noses.

"S'pose you're a bit like the mountains too," Declan said.

They stared down at him, agreeing without words.

"That's what makes you so smart," he went on. "Sometimes it's easier to see things more clearly when you're higher up. I think that's what helped me see that I had to let Jaz and the others go so we could all be free."

If time had been important to them, the heads might have wondered at the speed of a year's passing. But it wasn't. From where they stood, they had witnessed the sun rise and set too many times to notice. They had watched the phases of the moon and had even had time to count the stars. And with each new dawn, they had seen the world renewed regardless of what small events of life and death happened elsewhere. It was as if just *being* was enough for them and everything else of little consequence.

Time had dulled Declan's pain. It had helped mend his bones and heal the outward scars, although the doctor had said he would always need to be careful of his ankle. Time had even silenced the whispers and ended the secret, sideways looks as he had, inevitably, become yesterday's news at school.

A year had passed and he had come to say goodbye. It was time to move on again. To another place, another city. A fresh start.

"I thought I might find you here," Miss Everett said.

Declan turned to find her standing behind him, watching. He noticed the copy of the *Vancouver Herald* in her hand and looked away. They stood for a while, side by side, just hanging out with Charlie, Big Bird, and Sad Face.

"It isn't over yet, is it?" he said.

Miss Everett paused as if unsure what to say, then seemed to decide the truth was best and shook her head. "The trouble with Jerry Redback is that he thinks he is always right and everyone else is always wrong," she said. "His mind is made up. The thoughts set in his head like concrete. It's too late to try and change him now. That would take a miracle."

"I must have made his day when I went over the edge," Declan said. "It was fly or die, everyone knew that." He smiled grimly. "Guess I let Mr. Redback down again."

Miss Everett took him by the shoulders and made him to look at her. "What you, Jaz, and the others did was wrong," she said, "but none of you deserved to die for it."

"I know that now—tell it to Redback!"

She sighed. "We all meet people like Jerry Redback wherever we go in our lives," she said. "That's why we've got to be strong. That's why we have to believe in ourselves and not what they say about us. Then they can't win. Not ever."

A yellow-and-black taxi arrived with his dad in the back. "Your mom called from the office," he called. "Better hurry. She's meeting us at the airport."

Miss Everett hugged Declan goodbye. "There are no easy answers. You know that, don't you Declan?"

He nodded and slid onto the backseat. The door closed.

"You're OK, *Polly*," he said through the open window.

She smiled, promised to write, and waved as they drove away.

Declan watched the streets slide by as the taxi took them to Vancouver International Airport. They parked by a beat-up Land Cruiser and loaded the suitcases onto a baggage trolley. The sliding doors hissed back and Declan stepped inside. He recognized the voice immediately.

"Big Foot!"

The old man was over by the refreshment stand, telling the girl behind the counter all about his great grandfather in a blatant attempt to wangle free food. He looked up and showed all the gaps in his teeth when he saw Declan.

"I could not let you go without saying goodbye, my young friend," he said, slapping a big, bony hand on his shoulder. The old man looked deep into his eyes and seemed to approve of what he found there. "Maybe in the fall, you could leave the big, fancy city and let me show you those bears fishing for sockeye in the Thompson River. Some of them are . . ."

". . . nine feet tall, I know," Declan said.

Big Foot laughed and pulled a letter from his pocket. It was from Manu, and Declan smoothed out the creases as best he could.

"S'pose she spends a lot more time helping in the shop since Mad Dog won the Pipe-Burner," Declan said.

Big Foot nodded. "There is always much work to do when there are only two of you, but now the one you call Mad Dog has gone to Whistler, their shop is doing much better. Of course, no one can prove he was stealing the stock, but Manu's father now sees that he judged you harshly and regrets it deeply."

A pause, then Declan shrugged. "It wasn't all his fault. I guess he was just trying to protect Manu."

Big Foot smiled. "You have traveled far from the moment I first met you, my young friend."

Declan's mother arrived. Hurrying in, ear pressed to her mobile phone. Some things never changed.

"What can we do?" Big Foot said with a sigh.

"We are all born with the Great Unrest. Maybe that's why life is a journey of understanding."

Declan was reading Manu's letter when the final call for their flight was announced. Quickly, he begged for a pen and some paper and began to draw. Gradually, the perfect shape of an ear appeared on the page.

When he had finished, he folded the paper and asked Big Foot to give it to Manu when he returned to Timberwolf.

Big Foot looked at the picture and frowned. "I have heard of lending a friend an ear," he said, "but this is perhaps a strange way of doing it, is it not my young friend?"

"It's a long story," Declan said and smiled. "Maybe I'll tell it to you sometime."